A Walk on the Other Side

SHORT STORIES

A.J. Hughes

Anicale Publishing—Madison, WI
ISBN: 978-0-9998967-9-2
Library of Congress Control Number: 2018933602
Title: A Walk on the Other Side
Author: A.J. Hughes
Digital distribution | 2018
Paperback | 2018

This is a work of fiction. The characters, names, incidents, places, and dialogue are products of the author's imagination, and are not to be construed as real.

DEDICATION

I would like to dedicate this to my mother, the one I admire most as a writer. And for being the one to encourage me to write.

I would also like to thank my siblings and stepdad for their support.

I would like to thank all the thriller, horror, and fantasy authors and screenwriters that inspired my interests in writing these kinds of stories.

And to my grandmother Janice M. Brent, who passed away before this was published. I wasn't able to say goodbye. (12/09/2017)

ALSO BY A.J. HUGHES

A Day of Rain

A Day of Rain is a collection of LGBT short stories about romance, heartbreak, loss, rejection and acceptance on rainy days and nights.

ISBN: 978-1-7334454-2-9
Release Date: 12/03/2020

A Life: Worth Living

Recently aged out of the foster care system, Maya moves to New York City for a new start on life. After little success, loneliness and depression, Maya decides to commit suicide when a fateful meeting with Daniel changes her outlook on life.

ISBN: 978-0-9998967-0-9
Release Date: 05/11/2022

TABLE OF CONTENTS

CHAPTER ONE
A WALK ON THE OTHER SIDE

The temperature was dropping, I left the cabin 3 hours ago. The blizzard was getting heavier, and it was hard to see. I was lost, I couldn't tell right from left. It was a mistake to leave. But it was spur of the moment rage. My wife was tired of me working all the time. We took a vacation to an expensive cabin up north with our 2 kids for "family bonding." Something my wife felt was important. But just because we were staying two weeks, didn't mean work stopped. I had an important project meeting as soon as I got back. It was put off accommodating her.

—3 hours earlier—

"I'm sick and tired of your excuses," Jannette yelled. "All you do is work. You can't even take a day to just be with your family!"

"If I didn't work as much as I did, we wouldn't even be able to afford this," I retorted.

"Bullshit! We could afford this cheap shit with the kids' income."

"And where does that come from? Me!"

"Oh, so I don't take part in their allowance?"

"No! I give you money, you don't work, do anything around the house, or even watch our kids for that matter. If I didn't work, would you step up to paying 30,000 a month?"

Jannette was silent.

"I didn't think so."

"I still think you're being very selfish. Maybe I don't work or take care of the house, but it seems I'm the only one invested in our family. When have you ever gone to Katie's piano recitals or Mark's kendo meets?" Jannette asked. "Don't lecture me because we have a nanny to help take care of them, you aren't even in the house to know what I do."

"I WORK, I can't slack off, or I lose my job. That's the real world, just because you want family bonding doesn't mean I can stop reality and have fun. I have two weeks' worth of work to do, let me finish it, damn," I sneered sitting down.

Suddenly, Jannette grabbed my laptop and smashed it on the ground, "Work with that!"

"WHAT THE FUCK!"

Instant rage built, and it took everything in me to not break something. And no, I don't hit things when I'm angry nor do I believe in hitting anything. Sometimes, certain things can make you go over the edge. The real strength is surpassing that anger.

I took a deep breath and grabbed my coat, a hat and a scarf and went to our children's rooms, "I'm sorry you had to hear that, goodnight."

After saying goodnight, I walked to the door.

"Where do you think you're going?"

"Any place but here," I said, opening the door. "Enjoy your family bonding without me."

"It's practically a storm out there what are you doing," she asked. "Bill, BILL!"

I heard her call my name as I walked into the soon to be storm.

I only wanted to be gone 10 minutes, but the storm grew stronger, and soon I didn't know where to turn. It was very cold, maybe 10 below? The wind was probably 30 mph. I could barely walk, let alone breathe. My movements grew stiff, and my pace slowed.

"*Is this where I die?*" I thought dropping to my knees.

I placed my head on the snow and closed my eyes. The wind stopped blowing on my face and I opened my eyes. There I saw a door. It was white, with cracks, chipped and worn-out paint, and the doorknob was rusted. It looked like it hadn't been used in years. I couldn't see the surrounding walls, but I figured it was because of the snow. With my last bit of strength, I limped to the door and opened it.

When I opened the door, the warmth of a soft breeze welcomed me. I looked inside, it was astounding. On one side was a blizzard, on the other, a warm spring day.

"The décor in this house is impressive," I thought, all the fatigue in my body gone. *"I'll stay until the storm eases up, then I'll head back."*

Before closing the door, I saw a black shadow that looked as if it were being sucked into the door. Once it was gone, the snow surrounding the house disappeared. It was weird but at the time I just figured it was my own shadow and the heat from the house, made it melt. I closed the door and turned around. The house was really impressive, as I walked around the room, it looked real. The animals, the trees, the river, all of it. I continued into the "forest."

The "sunlight" was hot, "How did they get these lamps so hot?"

"Not lamps," a voice said. "The sun. Lamps not that big."

Startled I said, "Who's there? Sorry to intrude into your home. The storm was really bad."

"Home? Forest not my house. My house pass river."

"What do you mean river?"

"Over there, follow, follow."

The thing was tiny and green. It looked like a green fairy flunky. She was honestly quite beautiful. Or at least I thought it was a she. She was small, maybe 5 feet, slender, with a tiny face and big black eyes. She dressed not how a stereotypical fairy would dress, but like a Christmas elf that didn't get into beauty school. I was enticed by her as I followed her, her small legs barely making progress.

As we walked deeper into the forest, the trees became dense, and the "sky" disappeared. It grew dark, and just a short distance ahead was a soft light.

"My house there," she pointed. "Come come!"

She pulled at my wrist and ran to the cottage. When we arrived, it was surprisingly big for such a tiny person.

"You make self comfortable. I bring food and drink," she said, running into the kitchen.

I sat down on the sofa, the room was wooden. Everything had a wooden design.

"Are these all handmade?" I asked, running my hand across the side table.

"Handmade?" she asked with a look of confusion. "All things here made by hand. How else make?"

"Well, I would buy mine from a store."

"But thing from store handmade too."

"Not always, machines make most of it. They have to make thousands of furniture sets. Each by hand would be impossible or very time consuming and hard."

"What is muhsheen?"

"A machine? A robot, something built by man, strong, mechanical, not alive."

She just stared as I tried to explain so I gave up.

"So why here?" she asked jumping next to me on the couch.

"Well," I said, sliding over. "I almost died in the blizzard. Then I saw your door and walked inside."

"What door? My door here, you far from here."

"Yes, but I mean the front door. The door leading to your house."

"Don't understand, no door to lead to forest. Don't know what blizzard is."

"A blizzard, you know, from snow? A really bad snowstorm."

"No snow, it spring. Snow gone."

"Look I know where I was and how I got here. You can play pretend forest fairy all you want, but I'm getting out of here," I said, storming out of the house.

"Wait, where going?" she said, yelling out the door.

"To find the door."

"But food!"

I walked back to where I met the "fairy," but all signs of the door were gone.

"Wait, I just saw it. I know for a fact it was right here," I said, panicking. "Please don't tell me I'm stuck in this place?"

As I thought that, the flunky fairy showed up again.

"Find door?" she asked.

"Not yet," I said, avoiding eye contact.

"No door here, door in mind."

"It's not," I said, frustrated. "How else would I have gotten here?"

"You walk from other forest."

I took a deep breath and walked away, *"The door's gotta be here somewhere."*

I searched until the sun set, no sign of the door.

"How could that be? I was sure I went through a door, that I was in a blizzard, that I just had a fight with..." I paused. *"What was her name? Jane, Jamie, Jannate..."*

I stood for a while. I'd forgotten my wife's name. After 5 minutes, it snapped.

"Jannette," I hollered.

"That was weird," I thought. *"Why did it take so long to remember someone I was married to for years?"*

Just then a woman appeared from a bush on the side where the door was. She was absolutely stunning. Prettier than flunky, drop-dead gorgeous. She was tall, approximately an inch shorter than me, her skin was a pale green, her hair was white and long, her body slim but curvy. Her lips were full, with a heart shaped face, if it wasn't for her alienlike eyes, I would have been in love. Her eyes were large, pitch black and oval shaped. But in a way, it suited her face.

I stared in awe as she walked towards me.

"Are you Bill?" she asked, her voice was low and pleasant. Ecstasy to the ears.

I nodded.

"It's nice to meet you," she said. "I have waited all my life for you to come."

"Well, that's nice and all but this is the first I've seen you."

"And I you," she replied. "It is said in the books a man named Bill will come to me on this day."

"And because my name is also Bill, you assume it's me?"

"Yes, it is said he would come through a door, and we would wed."

"Wed?!"

What was she talking about? The moment she said "wed", I snapped to my senses.

"What do you mean 'wed', we just met, and I'm already married."

"It is normal for a man to have more than one wife, stay with me tonight," she said, she dropped to her knees and grabbed my hand. "You needn't worry about anything. I am yours to serve you."

"S-sure," I said, my cheeks turning red.

I stepped away and continued, "What is it that you want?"

"I wait for our marriage."

"We just met, there's no way marriage is even an option. I'm a one-woman man."

"Please, come to my cabin, if it is not to your standards then you may leave. But please give it the night to think."

I sighed, "Alright one night."

She smiled, and said, "Thank you."

"You know," I said. "It'd be nice if I knew the name of the woman who just proposed to me."

"Do not worry about my name, you will know once we are married."

"Right," I slowly replied.

As I followed her, I saw flunky with a worried look on her face.

When we arrived at her cabin, it was like a cabin from a fairy tale. The wooded background, with the pond surrounding the home, and the butterflies and birds flying around.

"Do you like?" she asked.

"It's nice," I replied.

"That is good. I want your home to be of your liking."

"Right."

"Please, come inside."

When I entered, the fireplace was lit, the furniture was soft, and there was an aroma that seemed to relax my muscles.

"I will make dinner," she said. "I am sure you have not eaten during your travels."

"No, I'm fine," I replied. As I said this, my stomach with perfect timing growled. I chuckled, "Well, now that you mention it, maybe a quick bite."

"Yes," she said, lowering her head.

I waited there, silently as she cooked when a little tiny head popped up from the window. It was flunky, she beckoned for me to come. I looked to the kitchen to make sure the woman didn't see her and walked outside.

"What are you doing here," I asked.

"Came to warn," she whispered. "Esmerelda dangerous. Bad lady, run away."

"What do you mean 'dangerous?'"

"Not good lady. Eat Bill. Run away."

"Bill?" Esmerelda called. "Your food is ready."

"You no eat food. Eat 5 times and you never go home. You Esmerelda's food."

Flunky ran away as Esmerelda opened the door.

"Is something wrong?"

"No, no, everything is fine. I just needed some fresh air is all."

"Oh no," Esmerelda exclaimed. "It is the candles?"

"No, I just...every so often I need to go outside."

"I see," she giggled. "Come inside, I have prepared your meal."

Esmerelda prepared a feast. On the table was a turkey, stir fried vegetables, rice, cranberries, a pie, a roasted pig and that was just the beginning.

"It looks delicious," I said.

"Thank you. I will make your plate. Would you like wine or beer?"

"Either is fine," I said.

I looked with excitement at the amazing meals in front of me and remembered flunky's words.

"But one meal isn't going to hurt," I thought. *"I will just have to avoid the other four. Though whatever happens is the least of my worries if I can't find the door."*

I scarfed the food down and felt a little lightheaded. The room began to spin and in a snap, the room was back to normal, and I was fine.

"Food coma maybe?"

After dinner, we talked about our hobbies. Even though I knew her name, she refused to tell me. We talked until it was time for bed.

"This is your room," she said. "Though we are soon to wed, we must sleep apart. But to make up for it, I will bring a little snack."

"I'm fine."

"No, I insist."

"I'm fine. Dinner filled me up."

"It is a custom here for people to eat before bed. If we are to wed, you need to follow these customs."

"Right," I said, nodding as I walked to the bed.

"Great, I will be back."

"It's a snack. I doubt this counts in the five times," I thought.

Esmerelda came back with a tray of sweets. 15 cookies, 30 pastries, a strawberry shortcake, and a glass of warm milk.

"That's a lot for a before bedtime snack."

"Yes, I want you to be full. I do not wish for you to be hungry in the night."

"That makes sense," I said, taking a bite out of the cookie.

The cookie was soft and sweet. I never tasted one like it, and I began to eat every cookie with a sip of milk between every bite. My mind was on a rampage. EAT! EAT! EAT! It said as if there were no tomorrow. My mind was worried something would snatch this delicious food from me. I wouldn't allow it. I went on to the croissants, next the streusels, and the strudels, until there was only a few donuts and the shortcake left.

The donut went down rough, and something felt different. I looked at Esmerelda, the expression of satisfaction across her face made my stomach sink.

The once delicious crème filled donut was now a tasteless mound of dough.

"*What have I done?*" I thought sitting the donut on the plate.

"Do you not like it?" she asked startled. "Should I make something else instead?"

"No, it's fine."

"But I made so much, you must eat. I don't want this to go to waste. I don't eat much sweets, but I really enjoy baking."

"Honestly, I am full," I said, after finishing the milk. "I don't even know if I can continue."

"Oh," she said, disappointed.

"Yes, I really don't think I can continue. It's a custom where I am, not to eat before bed, I don't want to get fat. And I should already be in bed and asleep. I'm already passed my preferred time."

She paused before saying, "Being fat isn't a bad thing. You'd still be a handsome guy."

"Um, yeah. Nothing wrong with being overweight, I just prefer to be healthy is all. I need to get to bed, it's pretty late as is."

"I see," she nodded slowly. "Well, goodnight."

"Night."

I needed to step up my game.

The next morning, I woke to a fantastic smell. And Esmerelda entered the room.

"Good morning," I said.

"Good morning, on today's menu...I made quite the breakfast, one I have not perfected in forever. I hope you enjoy."

"Oh, thank you," I said. "But I'm not a breakfast person. I get sick for the rest of the day."

"Oh really," she paused. "But I went through all of this work to make your morning better. Surely, you don't want all my hard work to go to waste?"

"I can't eat. I don't want to get sick, I really appreciate you doing this, but I can't."

This was getting dangerous, I definitely didn't want to be killed but as a man, hurting a woman was uncalled for. I could die and save my pride or survive. It was a tough call, but I chose living.

I continued, "Maybe you could give it to your neighbors?"

Esmerelda looked confused.

"Where I'm from, offering food to the neighbors is a must before marriage. And I won't consider until it's done."

"Really," she nodded and smiled. "Then I better head over."

"Hurry," I said, hastily.

Esmerelda ran out of the room with the cart of food. It was a delicious smell, my stomach grumbled in protest. I couldn't trust her food, so my only chance was to find it in the woods. Maybe flunky's place. I had a few questions to ask anyway.

I got dressed and snuck out. Esmerelda must have been in the neighbor's home, it was the perfect moment to escape. I walked around to check for Flunky's. I had a good memory, so it was easy to memorize where everything was.

I ran through the woods until I saw the faint little light.

"*THERE!*" I thought picking up the pace.

I banged on the door, and Flunky opened the door.

Half-asleep she asked, "What want. To early, need sleep."

"I need you to tell me about Esmerelda."

At the shock of the sudden request, Flunky was wide awake.

"Come, come," she said, beckoning me inside. "What want to know?"

"I need you to tell me about her, what happens when I eat all of the food? Are there symptoms, or a time frame for this? Just tell me everything."

Flunky nodded, "Okay, sit."

I sat down on the sofa and flunky sat next to me. My stomach gave one last plea for food and flunky heard the tiny sound.

"I bring food, we talk after."

"Sure, thanks."

As Flunky cooked, I took a closer look around her living room. It was kind of barren. Compared to Esmerelda's, which was very homey, hers was worse than a bachelor's pad. What once looked like a wonderful wooden cottage home was now an ugly, drab, desolate environment. I wondered if she ever got lonely there. The room was a mess, broken bottles were spread around the room, dust and cobwebs cluttered the corners, and the windows were broken. Chills ran down my spine, and I decided to distract myself from the mess. I peered out the hole in the window and gazed at the scenery. At least her surroundings were pretty.

Flunky came back with a tray of food. They were tiny proportions, something for someone her size. I picked up the tiny hamburger and took a sniff. Compared to Esmerelda, it didn't smell as good.

Flunky must have noticed my reaction she stared before asking, "Something wrong with food?"

"No, I'm just surprised at the size of the food."

"I sorry, I only cook for self, I not use to cooking for others. I make more, if don't like."

"It's fine, this is good. I can't complain going into someone's home receiving free food."

I took bite out of the burger, and it tasted bitter. The taste of the buns was bland. But I didn't want to disappoint her, so I continued to eat. After I finished, I turned to Flunky and said, "Tell me about Esmerelda, what is she? And how does this whole food eating process go?"

"Esmerelda is forest Nymph, they dangerous creatures. They feed men and sometime women as way to make marry. You forget everything, and no go home for you. They eat man after give false security."

"And what is the process for all of this?"

"First you dizzy, then you lose taste, then you forget little thing, then you forget important thing, then you forget everything but Esmerelda."

"Okay, and how can I stop her?"

Flunky shook her head profusely. "No way to stop Nymph. Nymph scary creature when angry. Only way, you run away. You stay here, that it."

"What, so Esmerelda can't beat you or something?"

"Wrong, Esmerelda no attack me. Against rules."

"What rules?"

"Rules of forest, Nymph not allowed to attack me."

"And why is that?"

"Just rule, I don't go in Esmerelda house, she no go in mine."

"And you won't explain why?"

"It long story, forest history."

"And how about her name? Why is it you told me her name, but she refuses to tell me?"

"Because man not suppose to know forest name, you know our name you have power. I tell you Esmerelda's just in case."

"So, what exactly can I do with this 'power'?"

"You have control over Esmerelda, Esmerelda not attack you. But you forget everything you forget her name."

I paused to intake what 'magical power' I had over her and said, "Alright, I better head back before she figures I'm here."

"Why leave, you stay here. She get mad, but don't do nothin', rules," Flunky said, grabbing my arm.

Carefully, I walked out of Flunky's home and walked 'home'. When I arrived, Esmerelda sat on the dining table with her hands covering her face.

"Are you okay," I asked, softly but weary.

"I provided everything for you. I tried to be the perfect fiancé yet..." she paused. "You were seeing that Sprite behind my back."

Esmerelda burst into tears, and I panicked. "You got it all wrong. I went over there to thank her for yesterday. She helped me with something."

"You need to be careful," she said, breathy then calmly, "Forest Sprites are dangerous. They are quite cunning, and very deceitful. Especially Maurelle, in her first appearance she looks very sweet, delicate, and innocent. She pretends to be the heroine, but she is evil."

"How is she evil," I asked.

I obviously didn't trust her, but some information came of this.

"She eats men," Esmerelda said. "She will feed you only two meals, and you will be under her spell. Once that happens, Maurelle will devour you."

I was treading on dangerous waters, but I asked hesitantly, "Couldn't the same be said of you? Don't you feed me large sums?"

"I do it to show my interest in you. I simply want marriage. I am a Nymph, we do not eat meat. Or food in general," Esmerelda said, standing up. Esmerelda scoffed, "Can I take it, Maurelle *informed* you I was a man-eater?"

"Possibly," I said, evasively.

"I cannot believe you chose a *SPRITE* over your soon to be wife."

"Well, she was the first person I met, and she didn't do any outlandish things."

"She didn't offer you food?"

"N—" I remembered. Flunky...or Maurelle technically, did in fact cook a meal, I just ran out too fast for her to give it to me."

"And from what I saw earlier, you ate one of her meals. Was it tasteless?"

"A bit," I said.

"I figured," she nodded and turned away. "Maurelle is using that trick this time."

"What trick?"

"Maurelle has a little game she plays with humans. Us Nymphs seek to find a mate, and Maurelle will tell each one, 'The whatever number of times you eat blah blah's food, it will be tasteless.' And since she knows you have eaten two of my meals, she purposefully made it disgusting."

"And how do I know it's true? The second meal after eating the donut became very bland."

"That was just your nerves. I can cook you another meal to prove it."

"Alright, let's do it."

"And afterwards, I will give you a necklace. It will show you Maurelle's true form. You will see who was right, before it is too late."

I nodded, it was hard to figure out who to trust. "Maurelle" was the first person I met, and nothing happened to my knowledge. She even gave me the run down on how Esmerelda worked and those "rules."

However, I spent the night in Esmerelda's home, if she really wanted to eat me she had her chance rather than make me eat food to forget everything and then be devoured. In this situation I wanted to believe Maurelle. But after seeing her home, tasting her food, and Esmerelda getting everything she told me correctly, I decided to believe Esmerelda.

Esmerelda finished making the food. It was a smaller portion, with only three dishes, ham, vegetables and rice. She was eager to prove Maurelle wrong. I took a bite out of the ham and it was delightful. The consistency throughout each bite was perfect, I moved over to the vegetables and the rice. I wasn't much for eating plain white rice, but I topped it with the vegetables, and I couldn't stop. Esmerelda's food even after eating it the second time, was satisfying. Maurelle's food was purposefully gross. Esmerelda had proven herself trustworthy and I could taste in her food, she really tried.

After what could be considered dinner, I sat in silence as Esmerelda cleaned the dishes. All of this was hard to sink in. I watched Esmerelda working diligently and smiled. She really did look like an alien. Nymphs in fairy tales were always the beautiful women, with the foresty accessories, wearing the green leaf dress and beautiful eyes. Whereas Esmerelda was still beautiful, but she was different obviously. Her eyes were a bit creepy, but it matched her perfectly. I wondered as I stared, why hadn't I noticed this before. Maybe it was because of Flunky's cheap tricks.

"So, you said something about a necklace?"

"Yes, once I am finished here I will prepare it."

We sat there for a little longer before heading to the living room. I couldn't help but think I was forgetting something. And I felt a little guilty for it.

Esmerelda brought out a cauldron and a cart of different items.

"These items put together will show Maurelle's true form, as well as protect you from anything she tries to do. Do not let her deceive you again."

"Sure," I said.

Esmerelda placed the necklace around my neck and walked away.

"Where are you going?" I asked.

"I am going to rest. I want to make you another bedtime snack. But there is much to do later. Maurelle cannot be trusted at night."

"Why is that? I heard there was a rule between Nymphs and Sprites. You weren't allowed in her area and she in yours."

"That is true to an extent. The rules stand true. However, the rules do not necessarily have to be followed. I follow the rules as Nymphs believe in law and order. Maurelle does not. That is why she believes I will not enter her home, but it does not mean she will not enter ours."

"So, you're sleeping now, so that when she enters you will be ready?"

"Yes, I suggest you sleep in my room. She will not be able to approach you."

"That's a good idea."

We said goodnight and went to bed.

I woke to the sound of a door closing. Esmerelda was gone. I stood up and walked to the door. Carefully, I quietly cracked it. There stood Esmerelda and a creature. It was small and green. Its ears were pointy, boils covered its flesh, little hair was on its head. It was ugly and scary. I looked away and listened closely.

"I figured you would come."

"Where Bill?"

"He left. He will not fall for your lies anymore Maurelle. It is over."

"You lie too. You make Bill your husband. He forget his life before."

"I did not lie to him, you are the one here to devour, I am here for marriage."

"And what happened to your other husband? Did he run away, or did you kill him?"

"Neither, humans do not live as long as we do. They are frail creatures."

"Exactly more reason to end human's pathetic life faster."

"I see your speech is returning," Esmerelda said. "Do not get use to it, for once again you have broken the treaty between us. And punishment will follow."

"We will see who is punished. I will have Bill. We shall bet, who will win."

"I do not believe in a bet against my soon to be husband. You will have to fight hard for him. Now please see yourself out."

Esmerelda turned towards the room. I closed the door and ran back to the bed and closed my eyes.

After hearing their conversation, it was easy to tell who was more so on my side, neither could be trusted completely but they gave each other out. I needed to escape, but I had to figure out how.

The next morning, I woke to a delicious smell. Esmerelda once again made me breakfast, this time also smaller portions. On the plates were scrambled eggs, bacon, muffins, toast, and a pitcher of orange juice. She took out two plates and served us both.

"I thought Nymphs didn't eat."

"We can live with or without food. I prefer not to, but I want to prove nothing is wrong with my food," Esmerelda said, taking a bite of eggs.

Cautiously, I took a bite from the bacon, and then the eggs. Soon I was eating like normal. We finished breakfast and headed to the living room.

"I need to take a walk," I said, putting on my shoes.

"Okay, the necklace will help you if Maurelle gets close."

I walked out the door without giving her a response. I walked to the forest center where I came through. I remembered my goal was to find the door. I looked in bushes and in ditches, it was nowhere to be found.

"How could a door just magically disappear?" I thought. I wasn't going to give up, so I continued.

I walked in a direction I hadn't gone before, and I came upon a clear field. In the distance was the door. I heard the bushes behind me rustle and out came Maurelle.

"You can't go to door. Door too far, come with me. I save you from Esmerelda spell."

"Not working," I shouted.

"She's lying," Maurelle shouted. "You under her spell, she Nymph witch. You goner if you don't come with me."

"And why should I believe the deceiving man-eater?"

"You have better chance with me than witch Nymph."

"Fat chance," I snarked and ran into the field.

Esmerelda walked from behind the door. She chanted, and the necklace started to glow. Maurelle winced in pain and ran away. Everything went dark.

When I came to, I lay in Esmerelda's bed. I couldn't remember anything that happened. All memories of Maurelle and the door were gone. I could only remember marrying Esmerelda. How we came to meet was completely different.

"Good morning," Esmerelda said, carrying a tray of food.

"Morning hon," I said, giving her a smile. "What's on the menu today?"

"Today, not much but biscuits, a vegetable omelet, and apple juice."

"Sounds wonderful," I said.

As I ate breakfast, something felt off, I couldn't place where and why I was feeling strange, but it stayed in my mind forever.

CHAPTER TWO
THE GHOST

Since I was younger, I was told to never leave the house after 6 o'clock. The neighborhood kids and I were always forced inside by 5 o'clock and in bed by or before 6. My room was on the third floor of our house. My siblings and I shared a room and my aunt would make sure we were asleep. Our curtains were bolted shut so that we could not look outside. My father closed the doors and windows on the first and second floors and made sure the shades were dark and non-transparent. Not even a crack in the curtains was allowed. It was almost always pitch-black, if it weren't for the oil lamps. I was 15— the age considered grown up, when I was told why.

Every night ghosts appeared in our small town. Everyone feared them. They howled and cried for someone to help them. Each ghost came to a different street the next night or stayed on their current one. And the townsfolk in Lotterdale always talked about what happened on their street. That was the first night I could stay awake for when one came. Like usual, at 5 o'clock the kids were put inside, and the neighbors closed their doors and windows. My family and I moved to the second floor living room. I sat in anticipation on the floor, as time slowly came to 6 pm. And soon enough, the ghost appeared.

I could hear what sounded like chains scraping the ground, and it shouted, "Hello," it sounded distant. "Is anyone out here?"

It was a man. I could tell he was young.

"I don't know where I am," he continued his voice trembled getting louder. "I'm lost, hungry, and tired. Even just a piece of bread and water would be fine!"

I felt bad for him, "Should we help him?"

My father snapped his head towards me, "No! NEVER open these doors or windows!"

"Ok," I said, feeling a bit hurt. I returned my gaze to the window.

It wasn't really dark outside. I could still see the light coming through the curtains. Suddenly, a silhouette appeared, he was trying to peer in the house, searching for a soul to help him. The room grew quiet. Tension filled the air as the ghost continued,

"Please, I mean no harm. I'm scared, I'm lonely, I've searched days for a place to take me in. Please."

I glanced around the room. I could see the fear on my family's faces, my grandmother in my grandfather's arms, and my father still as could be.

I looked back at the window, the man stood there in silence for about a minute before he continued on to the next house. We sat there unsure of whether or not it was safe to talk, I was speechless. I wondered if we should check the windows to make sure he was gone.

"Dad, should we check to see if he moved on?"

"No," he whispered. "We cannot open the curtains. It's too dangerous."

"What would happen?" I couldn't understand why they were so scared.

He ignored my question, "We should all get some sleep," he stood up. "It's getting late, and we all have places to be in the morning."

Everyone agreed and headed to the third floor. My father waited for me to go up, he couldn't trust me. And I couldn't blame him, I was curious. And for him, that meant everyone was in danger. I guess. I walked up the stairs and glanced back to see my dad staring intensely.

"*Weirdo,*" I thought.

That night I sat there, it had to be about 2 am. All I could think about was that poor guy. Wondering the streets for food and shelter. I knew he was a ghost I just couldn't help but feel sympathy. Silence filled the room, and I could hear my thoughts loud and clear. The rooms were sound-proof, I couldn't hear a thing outside. As my thoughts rapidly came, I looked around my room. Growing up I never really thought about how the rooms were set up. My walls were navy blue, and my bed sheets, covers and pillowcase were all black. My room was bare, I had a dark brown bookcase with not a lot of books, and the door was painted dark red, my bed a little to the side of being in front of the window. I looked at the curtains, completely black, nothing shown through. It all made sense, so that these ghosts if they possibly got a peek inside, they would see nothing. Kind of irrelevant and unnecessary, I know. They were dead and can probably see in the dark or something. Who knows what my family was thinking. All I could think about was that man.

I looked back at the window, and a thought popped into my head, *"I wonder if he moved to another street."*

I got out of bed, and slowly walked towards the window, my heart was beating faster and harder. I grabbed a part of the curtains.

"Is this the right thing to do?" I thought about my father's words and paused, *"what's going to happen?"*

I took a breath and yanked the curtain open.

"Of course," I whispered.

The windows were boarded up, they probably figured at some point one of us would attempt to open the curtains.

I let out a sigh and headed back to the bed.

"It's probably almost morning. I should get some sleep anyways," I closed my eyes and fell asleep.

A couple hours later, my aunt woke me.

"Jane, it's time for breakfast."

"Mhm hm"

I got up groggy and got dressed. As I headed down to the second floor, I saw my father had slept on the couch. Talk about trust issues. I continued down to the first floor, we had a kitchen on the second floor, but we ate breakfast on the first. As I reached the kitchen, I could hear my aunt, uncle, and eldest cousin whispering. Sounded like an argument. I peeked around the corner to see what was happening.

"Look, we don't know what happened to her," my Uncle Brian said. "She disappeared. She's gone."

"I know, but—" my cousin James paused, his eyes were sad.

"Look we can't just believe what people say," Aunt Diane cut him off. "It's been 10 years. She's not coming back."

"But Dave on Streator said he heard her."

My aunt slammed the silverware on the counter.

"James, get it through your head. She's not coming back. She's dead," her back turned to the room. "We all saw it for ourselves, there's no way she's coming back."

Who were they talking about? What happened to her?

James sighed, "Dave said she was a ghost. Called out for help."

The room was quiet. The only thing heard was the stove.

No one knew what to say, I figured this would be the opportunity to come in. Before I could move my aunt started talking.

"Who knows," her voice was soft and low. "No one knows what happens when they're taken."

James and my uncle looked down at the table.

My aunt continued, "We can't just assume that she's suffering like those things. Anyway, we can't let Jacob know."

My dad? Why couldn't he know? I was confused, who were they talking about, and why couldn't my father know?

I wanted to hear more but someone was coming downstairs.

"Morning," I said, walking into the kitchen.

"Oh, good morning dear," my aunt looked delighted to see me. Of course, it was a fake smile considering the conversation from before. "I made bacon and eggs. And blueberry pancakes."

"Cool, can I have some eggs and pancakes?"

"I keep forgetting you don't eat meat. Coming right up."

As soon as I sat down my dad came in.

"Good morning," he said, tired.

My uncle and James flinched, a look of discomfort wrapped their face.

"Morning," James said. "You slept on the couch, your back probably hurts huh?"

"No, not at all. Sometimes you just got to sleep in a different place."

"Ha, what an awful excuse," I thought

Later that evening, Aunt Diane, Uncle Brian, and James were on edge. We waited for the ghost to come, but it was quiet. 30 minutes passed, and I could faintly hear the chains. This time it was a woman. She sounded frantic and scared.

"Help, I don't know where I am," I could hear in her voice she was crying. "I had a family, 3 kids and a husband."

She continued, "I lived in a 3 story house, with my entire family. I want to go home, but I'm lost. Please, someone open the door. I'm lost and hungry."

Her voice was weak, I felt bad for her. I took a peek at my dad. His face was pale, not blinking. He was shocked. I looked around to see if anyone else saw him. Everyone had uneasiness, fear, shock, or sadness on their faces. My father stood up and walked slowly to the window.

"Dad?"

He ignored me. He was in disbelief.

Uncle Brian got up and roughly pulled him away from the window.

"Get a hold of yourself Jacob," he took my father's shoulders. "It's not her, Julianne died remember? We all saw it for ourselves, no way that's her!"

"But," my dad paused. He could barely think straight. "But I can hear her, she's out there *crying* for us to help her."

"Then why isn't she saying our names?"

Dad stopped struggling. He sighed, "You're right. It can't be her. She died a long time ago."

He then sat back down but next to me, "Sorry you had to see that."

"It's okay," I said, as I leaned on him.

"I guess I should give you an explanation on what just happened," he said, chuckling.

"Yeah, that'd be nice. But later is fine."

After we knew it was safe my family went upstairs. Only my father and I remained. We sat in silence for what could have been minutes or a few seconds. My father's face was serious. I knew this was important, just from his look alone and his outburst when the ghost came. This was nothing to joke around with. After what I think was 10 minutes he spoke.

"I want to apologize for earlier," he said, looking to the floor. "That woman or thing sounded like your mother. The reason why we don't tell you about the ghosts isn't just because of them being scary for children."

He continued, "But because if those windows or doors are opened, they come in and take the one who opened it or the one closest to the window. They're attracted to the light, sound, and movement."

My father continued to look at the floor as he spoke.

"Your mother, Julianne, I watched her as she was taken. She felt bad for one of the ghosts, a child, and opened the window. Your uncle and I were the last ones to head up before your mom. We heard her start screaming, 'over here honey! You have a home here.' And the child came and snatched her."

His voice was weak as he spoke. I really felt bad for him. It sucks I guess that my mom was killed in a messed up way but I never knew her. I couldn't even remember her face. I never had a connection with my mother.

I didn't know what to say to him, after a moment of silence, he spoke again, "That's why I'm so harsh on you for doing that. I don't want you to go through whatever your mother did."

"Dad, you don't have to worry about it. I won't actually open the window for one."

"Your mother said the same thing."

"Well, I actually mean it."

"Promise me you won't."

"I don't ne—"

"PROMISE," he said, his eyes forceful.

"Fine, I promise," I was reluctant to because it was another method for saying that he couldn't and wouldn't trust my words.

"Good, you should head to bed."

"All right. Night."

As I headed up the stairs I could hear the woman calling again.

"Why won't someone help me? Please, I need to get back to my husband and kids," she was frustrated. "Look, I remember his name."

She paused for a bit then continued, "His name is Jacob."

I looked back at my father, his face was appalled.

"Look," I said, as I rushed back down. "She could be shouting random names, or it's just a coincidence."

"You're right, it's just a coincidence."

She continued, "I-I remember my kids. My eldest, her name is Jane, then Newt, then my youngest Lily. I remember them. Please someone help me!"

"Jane," my dad said in a whisper. "Go to your room and make sure everyone's doors are shut."

"Dad," I said. "You can't be serious."

He had a look of resolve. His mind was already made up. While I watched, I wondered if there was anything I could do to stop him.

"Dad, you told me never to open them. Don't you think you're setting a bad example?"

"No, actually. If you see what happens to me, you'll never go near the window, and you'll be more cautious."

"Yeah? Well, what about when you're gone? What do you think I have to say to Newt and Lily? That their dad is dead?" I cried. I never thought I would have to talk my dad out of basically a suicide attempt.

"What about this? Just like mom appeared again, what makes you think you won't? We'll have to think about this again, Lily might want to be with her father and go, or I'll regret this forever and later feel like I have to end your suffering. What about that?"

My dad paused and looked at me, "J, I've been alone and unhappy since your mother left. I live everyday with the regret I couldn't save her. I love you all dearly. But if I can save your mother right now, I will."

"I don't think it's possible to save her, it's not her. It's just a coincidence, it has her memories, it can't be her. It's been 10 years remember?"

Father took a sigh and said, "Jane, step away from the window. I don't know what will happen I just want you safe."

He continued, "When I'm taken, I want you to wait a second and close the window."

"Dad please," I managed to say.

I begged him not to do it, but he seemed convinced that was what he needed to do. I waited for some confirmation that he would turn back, but he just stared at the blinds.

"Jane, go."

I stepped away as he first opened the blinds. He slowly pulled the window open and leaned outside.

"Honey! I'm here," he shouted waving his hands.

Suddenly a ghost appeared illuminated in light. Its eyes were completely white, its white hair flowed as it came towards the window. A gust of wind rushed into the room.

"Does it look like her?" I shouted, shielding the wind from my eyes.

"No," dad said, as he looked back and smiled.

I looked into his eyes one last time, regret and disappointment filled them.

And in an instant a bright light flashed, and they were gone. I stood there unable to move. I was scared out of my mind, my brain knew I needed to close the window, but my body wouldn't move.

As I stood there I could hear the faint sound of chains, which snapped me back to my senses. I ran to the window, slammed it shut, and quickly closed the blinds before moving to the side. I could hear the ghost as it spoke.

"Hello? I know someone's in there. Please help me, I'm injured, and I can barely stand. Please."

I held my breath as it attempted to look into the window.

"Please. Why won't anyone help me?"

The image of my dad's last smile when he said it wasn't her flashed in my head. I slid to the floor and cried. It was silent, but powerful. I couldn't stop. It was hard not to make a sound as the ghost shouted for help.

Morning came, but I felt it was still night.

"Jane?" my Aunt said, coming downstairs. "What are you doing there?"

I looked up, my eyes were puffy.

"What's wrong honey?"

"Dad," I paused. My voice croaked, "Was taken."

She had this look of trepidation on her face, "What do you mean. This isn't a funny joke."

"I'm not joking," tears rushed to my eyes, but I held them back. "After everyone left, we talked about my mom. Then as we were heading up the ghost appeared again, she said our names, my fathers and her kids. And dad decided he was going to end her suffering and join her, I tried talking him out of it."

The last words were hard to get out before I started bawling.

"I tried so hard to save him, but he wouldn't listen," at some point Uncle Brian had come down while I was explaining. "He told me he was lonely and regretted not saving her. And then he opened the window and it wasn't even her! He died for nothing."

Aunt Diane sat in silence, and Uncle Brian walked over.

"It's okay," he said. His voice was gentle. "You did everything you could. Nothing would have stopped him."

"I know," I said, wiping my eyes. "It's still sad, especially because he died in vain. I still see the look on his face when he told me it wasn't her."

"It's okay," Diane said, holding me.

Later that day we held a burial for dad. It wasn't much considering his body wasn't there. But we put his photos and some of his clothing in a casket before we buried them. It was heartbreaking to see my siblings crying for dad. What was I supposed to tell them? They were too young to know the truth, but I felt it was wrong to lie. I barely spoke with them during the funeral or the wake.

A year passed, and everything seemed to have gone back to normal, except my eldest cousin James left the town and my grandfather became ill. It was more towards the death of my father that he became sickly, maybe it was the shock or hurt, but he was in dire need of medication 3-5 times a day.

One night, a little over an hour before 6 pm, my grandfather told us he was out of medication, said he didn't want anyone to have to go and get some.

"Father," Uncle Brian exclaimed. "It would have been better if one of us had gone earlier than having to leave now to save you."

"That is just it son," he said, as best he could. "I do not need to be saved. I will just die tonight."

My grandmother was already in tears but hearing him say he was going to die tonight, really made her cry.

"Look grandpa," I said, coming into the room. "I can run to the store as fast as possible and be back before the ghost even appears."

"That is out of the question," Uncle Brian said. "It is way too dangerous for you to go. I'll go."

Uncle Brian was the oldest of his siblings, he was 47, and in no way, shape or form could he run more than a mile and make it back before the ghost.

"Yes, but I'm younger than everyone else. And I can definitely run faster," I said, as I grabbed my bag. "The time you're wasting trying to convince me not to go is more time risking for the ghost to appear."

"Fine," he said, walking to the door. "But be back well before 6 pm. And if you can't make it here, stay where you are or go inside a neighbor's home."

"Alright," I said, as he left.

"Jane," grandfather motioned for me to come to him. "You do not have to do this for me."

"It's okay," I said. "I needed to go for a run anyways."

I kissed him on the forehead before leaving.

I checked the street before completely stepping out. Making sure no ghosts were there. It was quiet and made this even more nerve-wracking. Walking down that street was like being in one of those horror stories. It was creepy and disturbing. I glanced at my watch, 5:10 pm. I had time. I took a deep breath and exhaled. I started to jog before going into a full sprint.

I made it to the pharmacy within 9 minutes, it wasn't the best I'd done, but considering the immense pressure it was astounding. I walked inside to see only one worker and a line of 5 or more people. I stood behind a woman, no more than 5'3". She was tapping her foot impatiently and looking at her watch. It was understandable considering we were all in a rush to get back safely. I figured no one would be coming in so I grabbed a few items like snacks and water to take home. After about 15 minutes I finally reached the counter.

"Hi," I said, to the clerk setting down my items. "I also have to pick up a prescription for Donald Harper."

"One second," he said, turning to the wall of medication.

He was a rather slow man, took his time gathering each prescription. He worked as if he had not a care in the world. While the customers worried on what to do if they weren't able to make it home before 6 pm.

"Alright, here you go," he said, handing over the bag. "I'm telling everyone. But if you feel you won't make it in time, you're welcome to stay here."

"Thanks," I said, grabbing the bag. "I'm going to make it home. Have a safe night."

I walked fast out of the pharmacy and checked my watch. 5:39 pm. *I can make it.* I thought as I began to jog.

My heart raced as I ran down the streets and through shortcuts. *I can make it* was all that ran through my mind. I was close to home when my bag broke. Everything spilled out, water was busted, and the glass items broke.

"Crap," I yelled gathering what I could.

I looked at my watch, 5:53 pm.

"I can make," I said, this time out loud.

I ran to a sprint, my breath was weary. I only had a block to go. As I ran I looked all over to make sure nothing was nearby. At last I reached my home. Only 8 feet away, I heard the sound of chains. I glanced at my watch, 5:56 pm. It was early. I thought if I ran in quickly I'd be safe, but I knew that would put my family at risk. I sighed and threw the prescription on the window sill and throwing a bottle of water.

Brian looked out to see me. He opened the window,

"What are you doing get inside!"

"I won't make it, it's here. I'll hide in that ditch behind the house, I'll be fine."

"Be safe," he said, grabbing the medication.

I watched him close the window before glancing to my side, it looked like a man, he was tall and was floating through the street. Instinctively, I ran to the side of the house. The ditch was almost completely covered by a bush. I dived inside. I covered the open hole with my jacket and stopped moving. He was close. I could see its faint light through the crack in the jacket. I knew if I moved even a bit, it would find me.

"Please, help me," it shouted. "I saw you. I just need you to tell me where to go. I'm lost, and if I can go inside your home I'd feel safe."

I remembered this ghost. It was the man I'd heard the first time I was allowed to stay awake. I guessed he made his rounds before returning here.

The light appeared directly over my jacket and everything lit up. I froze in terror. Only my sweat moved down the side of my temple.

"I know you're nearby, please," it said, aggravated. "I want to go home, please come out."

It stood there for what seemed to me like hours. My legs tightened, and my back hurt from staying in this position for so long. I figured maybe if I moved just slightly I could relieve this stress and not be heard. I shifted my back and legs slowly, to the right, which was spacious. As my arm slid, the bag of chips I had crinkled just a little and I came to a short halt.

I closed my eyes and prayed that he hadn't heard it.

I opened my eyes once again to see its face directly in front of mine. It stopped glowing, so I wouldn't suspect it, it really appeared as a man. The only features that made it similar were its body and facial structure. Its eyes were white and his skin, hair, clothing were white and it had a bright slightly blue aura around it. It wore a creepy smile. Its eyes that once looked human became slits. They looked like orange slices.

"Found you," it said, delighted. "Now I can finally go home!"

A light flashed, and everything went black.

When I came to, I was cramped inside of a fleshy ball. I could see faint shadows through a little light and all I could hear were things talking. They spoke English.

"Oh, I can't wait for you to come out."

"Let's wait to find out."

"Only a few weeks left. You excited?"

"That'll be $30.50 ma'am."

It was uncomfortable inside of it. I couldn't speak. I couldn't breathe because of these strange fluids. I was attached to a tube. I constantly kicked and punched at the walls, but nothing happened. All of a sudden, the seemingly plastic film broke, and the strange fluid gushed out. I was under so long I couldn't breathe after it left.

I lost consciousness, only to wake jarringly to a man in a blue robe, and a mask. He had to be 10 times my size. I looked around the room. The room was unfamiliar, nothing like I'd seen before. I had no idea where I was. There were strange devices on the counters and everyone wore these blue suits. Was I abducted by aliens?

There were so many questions, but I couldn't speak. The large man handed me over to a woman and she wrapped me in a blanket.

"Congratulations," she said, handing me to another woman.

"Thank you," she looked exhausted but happy. "She's beautiful."

I looked from her to the man standing over her. He looked like my dad! I tried hard to call out to him. Why hadn't he noticed me? Wait it couldn't have been him. He was taken by the ghosts a year ago. Was he turned into one of them, or had something horrific happened?

"She's very alert for a newborn."

"Yeah, I was just thinking that."

A newborn? Wait as in a baby? How? I was once 16 and now I was a baby again. It hadn't made any since.

"What shall we call her?"

"Hm," the man said. "How about Jane?"

"It's perfect," the woman said, looking down at me.

"Julianne," the man said. "We should have another child if this is what it feels like."

The woman named Julianne laughed, "Not for another 3 or more years."

Time went by and I was able to move. I was a baby. I had no idea what was going on, or how any of this was possible. The things in this world were new to me, like "cars" and the "TV". I also had to relearn a lot of things. My father never remembered me, and as I grew older, I learned that this was the "real world".

Some people say they remember what it was like in the womb, but I remembered what it was like before the womb. In a world before we were even a sparkle in our dad's eye. As time went on, my brother Newt, and Lily joined me. They didn't remember anything either. But they resembled themselves in the other world. Another child came along, I had no idea who he was, he was 5 years younger than Lily. He was probably someone that would have been born if Julianne had survived long enough, or maybe one of my siblings had a child, who knows. But I doubt he would remember the town of Lotterdale.

CHAPTER THREE
DR. VOGEL

D r. Vogel was a kind and quiet man. He was 65. He spent his days helping those less fortunate and those unable to pay for medical treatment. Vogel devoted his life to helping others, and yet, though he was helpful, he was terribly misunderstood. To the village he was cursed. At the age of 8, he was struck with a horrible illness which would have killed any other child. But he survived. How, was unknown, and rumors spread. That he was protected by a ghost, or that he took the life of other children in order to survive, or he was actually dead and walked around as a vengeful spirit. He was shunned, the village outcast, even his parents feared their child. Vogel had only known loneliness. He didn't mind much. He wore a smile at all times, except when he slept of course and even then, it wouldn't be a surprise if he did.

One day while walking in the woods, Vogel came across an injured bird. It must have been attacked by a predator or from the storm that hit only a few days before.

"Poor guy," Dr. Vogel said, as he picked it up.

The bird was small. It fit right into Vogel's hand. The bird was beautiful. Vogel had never seen one like it. Its feathers were of the deepest blue, gradients of blue spread across its body. It was like looking in the ocean, and on the tips of its wings were shades of red like a bed of roses. Vogel was mesmerized. All he could think about was its beauty. The bird moved very slightly, and to Vogel that was a blessing and a sure thing it was alive.

"I better take him back," Vogel said, as he hurried back to his cottage.

Dr. Vogel took care of the bird, spent days making sure it was okay. Naturally, he took care of others in the meantime. But it was the bird he worried about.

"Please be okay," Vogel said, as he rewrapped its wings. "I hope you wake up soon."

Vogel knew nothing about what he was feeling. He never knew what it would be like to have another living being near for so long. He loved the bird as if it were his own child.

3 weeks came along faster than he noticed. It was time for him to pay taxes. Vogel went to the closest village. On his way home, the same villagers ran into their homes, grabbed their children, and whispered

about the old man who returned. Suspicion was in the air, what was he up to? Why was he there? Did he require another life? As the villagers looked at the man with disgust, he wore a smile. Vogel didn't mind. The fact he was even paid attention to was more than what he could ask for. Vogel looked at the sky and watched as the birds flew by. His thoughts returned to the poor bird that slept on his window sill. When will he be able to fly with them again? Vogel suddenly had the urge to head home as fast as possible. He picked up his pace on the road home.

Dr. Vogel was hopeful, had the bird woken while he was away? Is he trying to find a way out? Vogel's smile increased. As he walked home, he passed a man. He wore a cloth over his face and held his eyes down as Vogel passed.

"Good afternoon," Vogel greeted. "It's a lovely day."

"Yes," the man responded. His eyes still looked towards the ground.

Vogel smiled and continued to his cottage. When he returned the bird was still sleeping. Vogel sighed and went into his study.

A day went by and still no sign of the bird waking. Dr. Vogel was scared.

"What if he died? Is this my fault? Was I too late, where did I go wrong?" Vogel prayed.

"Please," he said. His eyes filled with tears. "I have never asked for anything. All I ask of you is to please let him survive. That's all I ask, just save him."

Dr. Vogel got up from the window and headed to bed.

The next morning resembled any other, the bird continued to sleep. Vogel was upset, practically depressed. There was no one in his care that had not survived. He put everything into saving this bird, into saving all of the people he encountered. Why was the bird different? Why couldn't something so frail live like he had? Was this truly nature, for those weaker than others to not survive?

Later that afternoon, Dr. Vogel had a visitor. A younger male about mid-20's, he appeared very sick, beaten and drenched in blood. And with a quickness, Vogel was there to help. Dr. Vogel thought his eyes reminded him of the trees that surrounded his cottage.

"Your injuries weren't that severe," Vogel said. "Your arm is broken, and you have very minor stomach bleeding. Take these for the next 3 weeks and you will be fine."

"Thank you, Doctor," the young man said, taking the medicine bag. "Usually people fear me. Turn a blind eye to whenever someone attacks."

The man continued, "Turning me away at their doors, running in fear. Really, thank you. If there is anything I can do for you as a way of gratitude—"

"No," Vogel said, as humble as ever. "There is no need to repay me."

"Okay," the young man said. "If ever you decide to seek something, I live in the old mill, by valley falls. My name is Johann."

As Johann left the cottage, Vogel returned to caring for the bird. Johann glanced back at the old man who caught his curiosity and the bird in his hands. Not in the slightest had he seen someone ever be kind towards him or any other in years.

"Is he okay?" Johann asked returning to Vogel.

"No," Vogel said. "He hasn't woken up in over a month. I've tried every possible way for him to wake but nothing's happened. I fear he's soon to die."

Johann watched Vogel as his eyes lowered in pain. Why was the bird so important? Johann took a sigh.

"There is a way," Johann hesitated.

"What do you mean?" Vogel said, a bit of hope in his eyes. "Please tell me. I'll do anything."

Johann stood in silence before continuing, "It would be at the cost of your life."

Johann saw the despair in Dr. Vogel.

"In order to save the bird," Dr. Vogel paused. "I have to give mine? Why?"

"It is equivalent exchange," Johann said. His eyes reflected trees blowing in the wind.

"Something must be given of equal value in order to obtain what is desired."

He continued as he left the cottage, "The universe cannot have a life start again without one ending. If ever you want to do it, you know where to find me."

Dr. Vogel sat there in silence. Was there really a way to save him? But at the expense of his life. Was it worth it? He thought of the people whose lives he had saved, and those in the future who would need him. Vogel never felt so conflicted. He looked down at the bird, its breathing was shallow. It was obvious the bird was soon to die. Along with a sigh, he knew what he needed to do.

Vogel left for the Old Mill. On his way, Vogel second guessed his decision. It was one life compared to the many he could save. But Vogel knew there were plenty of doctors to help them, they didn't *need* him. Vogel rarely had visitors, and he knew he was a last resort because he was "evil." He could see on the faces of those who came, that they feared him.

What purpose would he serve if everyone stopped coming? Vogel lived his life, 65 years. What more could he do? Each day he was alone. Only patients who needed medication came once or twice a week. At least someone recently born could have a chance at life.

Dr. Vogel reached the Old Mill and called for Johann.

"Johann! I've made up my mind. I ask for this one favor! Johann!"

And as he said his name, Johann appeared.

"Are you sure?" he asked, for once genuinely worried. "You'll die in return."

"Yes," he replied. "If it will save his life, I will give mine."

"As you wish. When you enter, go to the bird and there I will give your life to him."

Vogel and Johann returned to the cottage. There the bird rested on the windowsill. It stopped breathing while he was away.

"Are you ready," Johann asked.

"Yes," Dr. Vogel said, walking over to the bird.

Dr. Vogel got onto his knees and gently petted the bird. Johann observed. He never thought there would be a human that would ever give for another, especially for a bird.

"What a truly sad thing," he thought. *"Do only the kind die?"*

Johann walked over to Vogel, closed his eyes and rested both hands on the two. A slight light, golden, like the river of life, appeared over Vogel's head and over the bird's. Vogel watched the bird, his vision blurred but he refused to lose sight of it. As his eyes closed, and his heart slowly stopped, the bird's eyes opened.

Dr. Vogel was happy, happier than he had ever been in his entire 65 years of life. Finally, he found a way to genuinely be useful to someone. And with the sign of the bird's life, Vogel took his last breath, and entered into an eternal slumber.

CHAPTER FOUR
THE CREATURE

The house was quiet. Everyone but Alice was gone. She could hear the rain hitting the roof and the sound of thunder in the distance. She sat in her room, the fear of being alone pulled at her. She sat at her desk doing the paper assigned for English. She glanced around her room. She saw the black walls and red carpet. The posters of the boy band she loved stared at her. On her floor and shelves were stuffed animals. They were looking at her and chills went down her spine.

"Great," she mumbled. "I can't believe I chose such a creepy room layout."

She returned to her work. Lightning illuminated her room, and she heard a crash downstairs.

"What was that?" she asked herself.

She heard the footsteps of a stranger climbing the stairs. She knew it couldn't be her family, they wouldn't be back until midnight. She ran to her bed and went underneath the blanket. She heard a faint hum calling her name. Begging her to play as it came down the hall. She covered her head hoping it was her imagination. She heard the tapping of a hand knocking at her door. She prayed the stranger didn't realize the door was unlocked. The door knob turned.

She heard the faint creak of the door and the stranger hummed, "Alice, come to me."

The door half open, "Alice, I'm here to take you away."

The door opened, and lightning illuminated the room, and everything went black.

Alice woke to a strange creature sharpening its knife. Her arms and legs were chained pulling her in opposite directions.

"Please," she whispered. "Please let me go."

She cried.

The creature turned, it didn't have a face. Its body was white, and its clothes were torn, more like rags, the color black. There was no sign of a mouth, eyes, or nose. The creature stared, its body motionless. It continued to sharpen the knife. Alice glanced around the room. It was dark and wet. The smell of mildew crept into her nose. The room's walls were gray, the floor was concrete. She wondered where she was and how long she had been down there. She saw a small window on the top right wall; it was big enough for her to squeeze through.

She wondered if she could escape. Impossible.

Her ankles stung from the chains and she winced. She continued to look. Alice saw a fire. Above it was a pot, boiling full of water. She screamed. The creature turned, its entire body faced her. It clenched the knife, its hands shaking. It was obviously angry.

A slight tear came to where its mouth should be. It widened, and the creature's mouth showed. Its teeth pointy, its tongue was like a snake's. The creature screamed. Its pitch hurt her ears.

"Be quiet," the creature yelled. It inched closer the knife tight in its fist.

"Please, I'm sorry," she cried. "Please don't eat me."

The creature kept walking. It stopped in front of her, its mouth opened, and its tongue slivered across her face. Alice felt like barfing. Bile crept up her throat. Just then she heard her family's footsteps.

"We're in the basement," she thought. "If I scream, they'll definitely hear me."

The creature backed away. It continued to sharpen the knife. Alice prepared herself to scream. But before she could open her mouth, the creature was done. Alice was paralyzed with fear.

"*What should I do?*" She couldn't move. She cried as the creature walked toward her. Preparing the knife in its hand.

"No," she whispered. "Please no."

The creature crept toward her, Alice begged it to stop. The creature raised its arm and swung.

Six hours earlier

The creature was hungry. It needed some kind of prey. Animals weren't enough. It wanted more. It needed something better. That was when it came upon a mansion. In the yard were five people. They were sitting at a table eating and laughing. They all looked delicious. Fattening themselves for it. It needed a way to lure them in one by one. It watched them, studied them. But before it could do anything it needed a place to keep them. It thought about keeping its prey in the surrounding forest, but anyone would be able to find them. It looked around. Maybe it would be better to have it inside their house. It searched the building but stayed out of sight. It circled around the mansion and found a low window near the ground. It seemed like a basement. It opened the window and slithered in. The room was dark and moist. It looked abandoned. The furniture was covered by white cloth and dust. The creature walked around checking the room, seeing if there were any signs of use. The room was perfect. Now the creature needed to devise a plan to lure them in. It looked outside and realized they were gone.

"They must have gone inside," it said, slithering across the room. It crawled up the stairs and cracked the door.

"Well, you guys can go without me," it was the sound of a girl yelling.

"Fine! Stay here," a man said. "If you can't act your age then you don't need to go."

"Whatever," the girl said, as she turned around and ran up the stairs.

The others continued on.

"I just don't see what's wrong with her," said an older woman.

"Just forget about Alice," suggested a kid. "If she wants to be a baby about going to dinner with her fiancé's family then that's her problem."

The youngest stayed quiet, his eyes looked down.

"Alright, so let's all get ready to go," ordered the man.

"Yes," they all replied.

They left the main room. Leaving it quiet.

"So, they are leaving but one," the creature said. "Guess this Alice girl will be first."

The creature crawled back downstairs. It was happy. It was the creature's first time eating a human. It was good that the girl was small. That way, if it wasn't as good as any other meat it had, she wouldn't be much to finish. The creature waited. It heard quick conversations between the members of the family. It had 30 minutes before the family was leaving. It was a long wait. The creature cleaned the area it was going to use to cook and eat. 7 o'clock came and the family left. It also left the house to prepare the meal. It brought wood, a pot, chains to hold her and everyone else down. By the time the creature was done. It was already eleven. The creature liked what it had done to the place. It was quite fashionable, with a little twist of creepiness. It walked around the house and knocked over a vase.

"Crap," the creature said, annoyed. "Hopefully she didn't hear that."

The creature crept up the stairs searching for her room. It saw a light at the end of the hall. The creature was happy. It figured maybe it should scare her a little. It crawled down the hall. Making as much noise in steps as it went to her door. It thought of taking up the fear.

It called her name in a whisper, Alice. Alice. Alice. It walked to her door and heard her running to her bed. The creature was in glee. The whole situation sent a chill down its spine. It slowly turned the knob and called, "Alice, come to me,"

The door was opening slowly. "Alice. I came to take you away."

Just as the door opened, lightning filled the room, and the lights went out. Alice fainted. And the creature grabbed her and dragged her down the stairs to the basement.

The creature first chained up her arms and pulled her up. It then added the chains to her legs, and pulled her limbs apart, just enough so she wouldn't be able to move. It turned around and began sharpening its knife. The only thing it could think about was the aftereffects. What would happen to it afterwards? Would it be able to enjoy a different type of meal? Would it go on a rampage? As the creature was in thought, the blade getting sharper, it heard the girl begging it to let her go. It looked at her, tears streamed down her face. She looked defenseless.

It pleased the creature to know it could actually scare someone and eventually eat. It continued to sharpen the knife. Then the girl screamed. It startled the creature, causing it to cut its finger. The creature was angry. It turned around clinching the knife. It opened it's mouth and screamed. The scream was high pitched, and the creature saw the girl wince in pain.

"Good," it thought. It crept towards her, the knife getting tighter in its hand.

"Be quiet," the creature yelled.

"Please, I'm sorry," she cried. "Please don't eat me."

The creature kept walking. It stopped in front of her, its mouth opened, and its tongue slid across her face. The taste of her was delicious, something it had never expected to taste. It heard the footsteps of her family.

"I'm still good," the creature reassured itself. "I'm almost done."

The creature backed away. It continued to sharpen the knife. The creature was so close to being done. It could hear the chains. It knew she was going to try something.

"Finished," the creature thought.

It turned around and walked to her. It could see the terror in her eyes. But it only left the creature wanting more. It was time. The creature prepared the knife in its hand.

"No," the girl whispered. "Please no."

The creature raised its arm and swung.

The girl's body went limp. The creature took a bite, the taste of the girl's flesh was like nothing it had tasted before. It was almost heavenly. The creature could not stop until nothing remained of the girl. When the creature was done, it felt something was different. It looked in a dirty mirror across from the site and realized it transformed into the girl. Its faceless, colorless body had become just as vivid as all of nature. The creature was happy but could not give up the desire to finish off the family. It could hear her parent's upstairs calling for Alice. It was the perfect opportunity. It could then feast upon this fiancé that the child was mentioning. And continue on until that hunger that was created, stopped. It could hear them talking.

"Let's split up," the man said.

"Okay," the older woman responded. "The children can go to bed."

The older woman probably shooed them off. And the creature heard the footsteps of tiny feet going upstairs.

"Alright," the man said. "You look down here and I'll go upstairs."

"Okay," the woman said, her voice sounded worried.

The creature could hear the man going up the stairs. This was the perfect chance for seconds.

"Alice," the older woman called. "Where are you?"

"I'm in the basement."

Chapter Five
The Train

This was a story I would never forget. I was walking down a deserted path. A place I go to everyday after working part-time at my uncle's farm. I must have been worked too hard, my body was sore, and my head hurt. I lived in a small rural town, with a population of 1,000. Everyone knew each other. So generally, if there was an event, most of the people in this town would be there. Anyways, as I was walking, I noticed a train station on the left side of the road. It looked old and run down. Waiting at the stop was a girl. She looked about 10. She was small, her hair was brown, and she was wearing a brown dress that looked like it was from the Victorian period, around the collar was laced and white. She wore black boots that were muddy, and she held a small black handbag. Our town didn't have any train tracks. Our town was so small we didn't get any tourist and no one really left unless they were tired of rural life. It was strange. Something told me not to talk to her, but I couldn't let this go. I walked up to her, but she continued to look forward.

"Excuse me," I said.

She continued to look forward.

"What are you doing traveling by yourself?"

It was like she could not hear me. So, I tapped her on the shoulder, and she flinched. Her big, round black eyes looked frightened.

"Are you okay?" Why was she so scared? "What's wrong? There's nothing to be afraid of."

"Yes, there is," she said, her voice soft and shaky.

"So, what's scary?"

"He is going to come," she answered, looking off into the distance.

Who was she talking about?

She continued, "If I do not get on this train, he is going to get me."

"Who's going to get you?"

Suddenly a train came. I didn't hear or see it in the distance. I assumed it was because I was too focused on her. Just as it was pulling up the girl looked past me. Her face turned pale, and she shivered. I felt a slight chill run down my spine. I turned around to see a man who looked like he didn't belong there, or anywhere. But before I could look at his face the girl grabbed my arm and pulled me on the train.

"Why did you do that?!"

"He was going to get you," she screamed, tears running from her eyes. "He was coming for you and me!"

"Why?! Why would he be after you? Let alone me?!"

She stared at me with a confused look on her face. "You do not know? You are—"

Before she could finish a woman came over and the girls face lit up.

"Helen," the girl yelled, jumping into the older woman's arms.

"Why did you run off?" she asked, holding her tight.

She had a scar on her face. She must have gotten it from a really bad accident. The scar stretched from the top of her head to her right cheek. She also wore a brown Victorian dress, the same as the girl's. Her hair was brown, I couldn't see her eyes. She had bangs that covered most of them. It was strange, she also wore muddy black boots.

"Helen," the girl said, snapping me out of my daydream. "He does not know!"

"No?" She looked at me then back to the girl. "It is best right now not to tell him. It is against the rules."

Rules? What rules? And what wasn't she supposed to tell me?

"It was good that I pulled him on the train, right?" said the girl, she seemed better now than previously.

"Yes, it was. But he would not have been able to get him because he does not know. But at least he is safe when he does."

"Um," I said. "If it's alright, I would like to know what's going on and how I can get home."

"It is nothing. Just stay away from the man you saw. He is a bad person. And now that he has seen you and you have seen him, he is coming after you too."

"Right... Well I don't know how to respond to that."

"Well do not," the woman dismissed my remark. "My name is Helen, and this is Lucy."

She pointed to the girl, and she waved.

She continued, "You can sit with us."

"Right," I said, walking after Helen and Lucy.

We sat down in a private room. It was also for sleeping. It was spacious and on both sides were two bunk beds. And in front were seats. It looked nice, but it was best I didn't get too comfortable.

"So," I said, sitting across from Helen and Lucy. "How do I get back? How far do you think the walk is from the previous stop to the next?"

"Well it is quite the walk. But if you just wait on the train, it will go back."

"Really?"

"Yes," replied Helen. "But it will be a long ride. It goes around the country in a circle picking people up."

"Well then what's the point of me staying? If it's going to take a long time, then there's no point in waiting."

Just as I was about to stand Helen said, "Wait. You have missed multiple stops we are by now in another city. Maybe two have passed."

I sat back down and leaned against the window, not looking at either of them.

"I know you are angry, but it is for the best and it will not take that long. Trust me. It is shorter than it seems."

I glanced at her, she smiled gently.

For the next few hours we sat in silence. Lucy was asleep in the bottom bunk behind Helen. I never looked at Helen once.

"Are you going to bed soon?" she asked.

I finally looked over.

"Nah, I'm not that tired."

"Okay. Well I am going to bed. Do not stay up too long," she said, gently getting up. "Goodnight."

"Goodnight."

I watched as she walked to the bed. She had an elegant walk and good posture. I looked back out the window. Everything was the same. But at each stop and every turn I saw that man. Every minute that passed he stood there. But I never saw his face. It was creepy. No matter how much time passed or how many cities, he was always there. Eventually I couldn't take it anymore and decided to try to go to bed. I got up from my seat and walked over to my bunk. I pulled down a screen above my bunk.

As I lay there in bed, I wondered what they were talking about.

"What did they know? What wasn't I supposed to know? Why am I on this train? When will I be able to go home? Why is that man following us?"

With those questions in mind I fell asleep.

I woke to the train hitting a bump, almost throwing me off the bed. I was alone in the room.

I got up, drowsy, my body ached, and I had a headache. I headed out the door. I didn't see Helen or Lucy anywhere. Did they leave me? I looked around, panicking, going through each car. I walked into a car that looked like a diner. It looked too big to be just one car. The walls were black with red and yellow squares and the floor burgundy carpet. Almost every table was full and at a table in the corner near the other side of the car were Helen and Lucy. Just as I spotted them, Lucy saw me too.

"Hey," she yelled, waving her hand. "Over here."

I walked over and sat next to Lucy.

"Good morning. How was your rest?" Helen said.

"It was good. I'm still tired, and hungry."

"Well, then why not order something?" Lucy said, taking a bite of her pancakes.

Just then a waiter walked up. He wore an eye patch, he had multiple scars on every visible part of his body, and a red spot on his chest.

"What can I get'cha?"

"Scrambled eggs, pancakes and oranges juice?"

"Comin' right up," he said, writing in his pad, and walked away.

The silence was awkward, I sat there avoiding eye contact until I remembered that man.

"Can you please tell me why that man is always following me? And how he's able to be at every stop?"

Helen's face had turned very serious.

"I cannot. You will have to figure it out yourself I cannot interfere."

"Well how can I figure this out myself?"

"By just realizing," as she said that, she stood up and left, leaving me and Lucy behind.

"So, you got any pointers?"

"Nope," Lucy replied, taking a huge bite out of her food.

The man walked over and sat down my plate, it looked so delicious. He sat in the chair across from us.

"You guys are with Helen right."

"Yeah."

"I'm Kevin. What are your names?"

"My name is Lucy."

"I'm uh...I'm...I don't know..." What was going on? Why couldn't I remember my name?

The waiter looked at me confused. It didn't make sense.

"So, I assume you don't know?"

"Know what?! What is it that I'm supposed to know? Why can't you guy just tell me?!"

Why was this happening? I just wanted to go home.

"Well, they aren't allowed to. But I can," Kevin said, crossing his legs. "Well, I can help."

He could help? I didn't know who he was and what kind of "power" he had on that train, especially as a waiter with a stain on his shirt.

"I can show you something that you might find helpful. Do you wanna see it?"

"Okay. Can you show me?"

Kevin smiled and snapped his finger. And something appeared on the table. It was a newspaper. On the front page in bold letters read:

BOY FALLS OFF OF MILL

I continued to read:

On August 8th, while working at Fred's farm, Jake was told to fix a few bolts on his uncle's grain mill. At the time the mill seemed sturdy enough to hold. When Jake reached the top, he began to work, he continued for about thirty minutes when a few cows were scared and ran into the mill. Jake lost his balance and fell. He was rushed to the hospital but was pronounced dead upon arrival. He suffered from a fractured skull and broken spine. After the investigation, police found that more bolts were missing from the bottom and when the cows hit, they loosened one of the legs on the mill....

Before I could continue, red liquid dropped on the paper. I touched my head. I was bleeding, and my back hurt. It was hard to move.

"That was me. I died? I can't remember," I thought. "Wait, I do. I was working when my uncle's dog was let out and chased after the cows. I stood up to see what was going on, and the mill tipped. I fell and everything went black. It makes sense. I just appeared, walking on that road. It just seemed like any other day."

"Ah," Kevin began. "Now you have figured it out. And now the effects are beginning to surface."

"Help," was all I could manage to say.

"Nothing I can do. Don't worry it'll be over in about 30 seconds. We'll wait."

I had forgotten that Lucy was still there. I looked over, she was scared. Lucy trembled, a blank look in her eyes. I closed my eyes and let the pain continue. And when it was over, I could move.

Kevin continued, "As you can see, we're all dead."

He leaned back and spread his arms out.

I glanced around, and everyone had blood or some feature that symbolized they were dead. I looked at Lucy and she had a huge gash on her head, blood crept down.

"How?"

"Helen and I lived at an all girl's boarding school. She was one of the teachers. We were treated horribly. I was treated the worst because I did not have parents but only Helen was kind to me. And to her, I was like her child. One day I was beaten and decided to run away. Helen found out and said she would leave too. On the way to the train station we got into an argument, and I told her I hated her and ran away. Helen chased after me and I ran onto the tracks. I could not hear the train and I was hit. I found out that Helen was also hurt but survived, only she died in the hospital later. I wandered around until I was told to get on this train."

"Well now that you know, we can leave," Kevin interrupted and got up. "Please go back to your seats everyone."

Just as he instructed everyone got up and left. I followed Lucy and went back to our room. Helen was sitting there, staring out the window. As we walked in, she turned around.

"So, you found out. How do you feel?"

"I don't know, hasn't really sunk in yet."

"Well, sit down you might like the view."

As she suggested, I sat down and looked out the window. We were in the air, going up.

"We could not leave until everyone on the train knew they were dead."

"Where are we going?"

"Heaven." She smiled. "And that man, well let's just say he wanted us to go the other way."

CHAPTER SIX
INSANITY

He opened his eyes to see they were back. Their dark eyes wide and curious about what they had happened upon. He thought and prayed to anyone and everything that could hear him.

"Please make them go away. I don't want any more of this. I want to go home."

The boy was 8, he knew nothing beyond the room he was confined to. He loved his dolls and his friend Jake. You see, Jake was alive. He talked to the boy, comforted him, reassured him he was alive. Everything was good enough to the boy. He was content in that dark little space. He loved it. It was his home. It wasn't until his friend told him about a world beyond what he could ever imagine. Out of curiosity he agreed to leave that tiny space.

"They took him away," the boy thought, *"He's gone! I'll never see him again, why is this happening? What did I do?"*

The strange creatures laughed and snickered at the frightened boy. They enjoyed his fear. Took it in, internalized the quiet breaths of the small child that looked at them, still as could be.

"He looked delicious," they thought, each of their minds thinking of ways to make a meal of him. One imagined him roasting over a warm fire, another envisioned biting off each little finger and every toe. Savoring the tastes of what could be spectacular.

The boy could see the desire they harbored. And the fear crept even farther through his body. He was paralyzed. The boy only had his mind to help him. His breathing that was once quiet and still, began to increase in speed and sound. His heart beat fast. It kept going, faster and faster. His lungs agreed with the rhythm of his heart. The boy could hear it. He could hear his heart beat louder and louder. Ba-bum. Ba-bum! BA-BUM! He couldn't bear it. the child was losing his mind. If this kept going, he wouldn't know what to do. He felt he would die of shear insanity. The boy questioned how and why this could have happened. Thoughts raced through his mind. He could hear Jake and the other dolls.

"Get out of there!"

"RUN!"

"It's not safe"

"Stay where you are, you'll only make it worse!"

"It's safer to stay there."

"Don't listen to them, they're wrong. Run before they eat you!"

Their voices confused him. What could he do, what SHOULD he do? He longed for things he never understood. The boy wanted a mother to cradle him, tell him everything would be safe. He wanted a father to beat away the bad guys. The boy knew nothing but that room. Maybe he could make a mommy, he thought. Like how he made the other dolls, and Jake. As these thoughts raced through his head the creatures were getting hungrier and hungrier. They became impatient. Where was their leader, what could he be doing at a time like this?

Their eyes never left the boy, didn't want him to run away. Oh no, now that would be bad. Their food would be ruined, dirty and smelly. Their dark round eyes looked at him, it scared him. They knew it, he knew it. The child had nowhere to run. Why did he listen to Jake? He would still be safe in his room, away from others, away from this dangerous world he began to know.

"I trusted him," the boy thought. "I trusted him, and he left me."

The boy was restless. Fear struck him in every twitch, every breath, and every beat of his heart. The boy was furious, his sanity was slipping away. His breaths heavier.

"Jake led me here. And, where is he? Gone, left me here to die! He wanted my room for himself. Yeah," the boy chuckled. His thoughts became meaner, harsher. He loved Jake, he was his friend, he could never do anything nor wish anything harmful on him.

The child continued, *"I want to leave, why am I here? Jake wanted this place. He was the one who left through the doors every day to come here. Now I'm dead. They're going to kill me, eat me raw."*

His dolly Susie spoke, "Child, you must leave, it's not safe."

Molly, "No, stay. It's much safer. Any movement and they'll attack!"

To the child, hundreds of voices rushed through his head, what was he to do? Who was there for him? They certainly weren't.

"Easy to say," the boy thought. *"They aren't here helping. Why should I listen?"*

As what seemed like hours past, the boy's heart grew jaded. What was once there was gone. But what did it matter? He was going to die anyways. And as these thoughts rushed through his mind, the creatures looked away. They weren't paying attention. Their leader had finally come. A small fella, not even close to the size of the boy, however, their leader brought them food, helped lead food into traps they couldn't set themselves, they needed him. His figured seemed all too familiar. But that didn't matter to the boy. All he could think was whether or not he should run. His chest hurt, his breathing rough. He was going to do it, he was going to run. Hide from the things that were once looking at him with a craving for his flesh.

The boy counted to 3 and ran. The things shrieked, their minds all thinking the same, *"If it weren't for our leader, he would be in my stomach."*

The pursuit commenced. And so, would the child's sanity be gone forever.

The boy sped through the forest, he knew the way back. He remembered it. He loved to memorize everything, from the words his friends spoke to what he dreamt last. He knew to remember this path. But no matter how much he ran, he would be no match for his pursuers. He wasn't the average boy. He didn't run around, he was malnourished. No way could he out run those things that chased their meals daily.

They were gaining. He could hear their anger, their shrieks, growls and snarls. While running, the child saw a small opening underneath a rock and thought maybe he could hide there until they found something else. The child crawled into the tiny hole, it was small enough for him to just fit in. It was 10 feet long, 3 feet tall.

"Thank goodness," the boy thought.

He could hide for maybe an hour. Not even, maybe 30 minutes at best. But to him, that was good enough. Better in that small space than in their stomachs. He heard footsteps drawing near. It was slow but loud enough. Thump, thump, thump. That fear that had once resided, found its way to his mind and body. He saw its legs, they were black, it didn't have fur, but rather smooth skin with bumps every now and then. Those legs were enough to let the boy know he stood no chance.

"It found me, I'm going to die," the child thought. *"WHY!? Why am I the one to die? I was a good boy, I played quietly to myself. I listened to my dollies. I never told a lie, so why?"*

The child was crying, the creature was there. While the child's eyes were closed, it made its way down to the little hole. The boy thought it would be too small for them to fit through. The things eyes were delighted, its smile accompanied by those eyes that sent chills through the boy's spine. It stood there, bent over, probably thinking of ways to get him out of that tiny space. Or maybe it was so happy to have found the child alone, it couldn't move. But none of this mattered to the boy.

He wished this would all go away. That he could return to that small room, back to his dollies, back to where he knew he would be safe. The boy began to rock, slowly as he thought about the bliss he forsook for a taste of outside.

"That's why," he thought.

The child figured it was the room. The room was mad, that's why he's in this predicament. That's why Jake disappeared. Because they were bad boys, he left the room that nurtured him like a mother, protected him like a father. That small dark damp room was his parents. That room took care of him and his dolls.

The boy continued to rock, tears streamed down his face, he stared into nothing. He could only think, *I was a bad boy*. That was his resolve. He chose a dangerous world over what he considered his mother. And this was his punishment, his time out. She gave him everything he wanted, the materials for the dolls, books, that little cot in the corner. All her.

The boy muttered, "I'm sorry. I'm sorry mother, I'm sorry."

He continued to rock, as the creature carefully reached its arm into the hole, and gently wrapped its hand around the boy's legs. The boy rocked. "I'm sorry mother, I'm so sorry."

The creature slowly pulled him out, carefully so that his meal would not be damaged. And as the thing pulled him, the boy could only think of his punishment from mother and his apology was all he could say. As the thing dragged him through the forest, their leader watched. He watched the child dragged to a deserted place, where the creature could feast in peace.

CHAPTER SEVEN
THE ORNAMENT: PT. 1

I loved Christmas, the decorations, the lights on every street, in every house, and in every room. I loved the festivities, the joy that fills the air and the giving and receiving. Christmas was a time for giving and bringing peace to the world and being with those you love. I loved to put up the tree with my family. My favorite part was putting on the ornaments. It was so enriching, so invigorating. Every night when my parents were asleep, I snuck downstairs to see the tree I put up. There was my favorite ornament, placed in the same spot every year. I don't remember when my parents bought it, I just remembered four years ago, putting on ornaments and seeing it at the bottom of the box. The ornament was round, its color was blue with a gold strip that went around the center. Inside the golden strip there was a village. It was colorful and lit up after midnight.

The village was alive. The people carried out their everyday lives. There were no crimes, it was peaceful, *the* ideal town. I loved to watch them as they travelled. Every so often a villager would look up and wave, I smiled back.

My parents thought I was crazy. They watched as I communicated with the people. They didn't realize I heard everything. I heard them as they talked to the man, I saw every morning. His name was Charles Gommer, every morning he came wearing the same grey suit. You could tell he didn't take care of himself, but it was Christmas, no judgments were allowed. Anyhow, they always told him I was getting worse, and every time he responded, "It's fine. Every kid has an imagination. There is nothing wrong with her psychologically, but if you push away her imagination, there will be."

I knew they were real. I *saw* them. Just because no one else could, didn't mean they weren't alive. I wished I was there, in that village.

Every night I prayed to God to let me stay there. I begged the villagers to tell me how to live among them, to be in that ornament.

Supper had just finished, and I went straight to the ornament when my parents headed to bed. I peered inside the ball and a villager was walking pass. It was a little girl, maybe 8 years old.

"Hi there," I said.

She looked up. I could tell she was frightened.

Giving a non-threatening smile, I said, "How's your day going?"

"Good," she said.

As I stood near the tree, my parents came down. They told me to go to bed. They threatened to break it, to kill the innocent lives that lived in that blue ball. And like all the other times, I went willingly, begging them not to break it.

I lay in bed, the room was quiet. I thought about life in that village. Oh, how wonderful it would be to be there, instead of in this world full of corruption. I closed my eyes and fell asleep.

I woke to an unknown ceiling. I was in a room I didn't know where. I got up and walked to the window. The lights were familiar. Outside I saw people walking and living in peace. I was in that village! With a burst of energy, I ran out the room-my room. This house was beautiful, the walls were burgundy, and the lining was white. The banister was made of maple wood. The carpet was brown. I headed downstairs. Everything was beautiful here too. The chairs were made of African Blackwood. The fabric was white. The table was Purple Heart. The side was carved with swirls that arched together in the middle on the long sides of the table.

I continued to glance around the room. There was a brick fireplace, the couch and loveseat were black.

"Good morning," a woman said. She was round and jolly. Her hair was blonde, and she had brown eyes. She wore a wide smile.

"Oh, good morning," I replied, as I turned around. "I love your house."

"Oh, why thank you. But this is your house too."

My house. MY HOUSE!

"Um, well, I should probably introduce myself. My name is-"

"Violet, I know who you are. All of us do," the lady interrupted.

"Heh, that's great. And your name is?"

"Oh, excuse my manners. My name is Norah."

"It's nice to meet you."

"And you as well. Why don't you go out and meet your new neighbors?" Norah inquired.

"Sure."

I walked outside. It was amazing. I looked up and saw the black that illuminated the sky. How was it bright, when there wasn't a sky? It didn't matter.

Everywhere I walked I saw smiling faces, everyone was so friendly. After about 2 hours of walking, I saw a sign: ***Transformation Park.*** My curiosity took over and I walked inside. It was beautiful. The leaves on the trees were red. Leaves fell from the trees leaving a trail. The leaves covered the cobblestone ground, and the two wooden benches across from each other. I walk down the trail. The wind blew harder and harder as I continued to walk. I saw a huge tree. Its leaves were multiple colors.

"Hiya," a stranger said, behind the tree. "Haven't seen you around."

"I thought everyone knew me. I'm sorry. My name is Violet," I stuck out my hand.

He took it, "Nice to meet you. I'm David."

David had black hair. He was skinny, and his eyes were green. He was actually kind of cute.

"So," he continued. "Where'd you come from?"

It was kind of awkward. I pointed to the sky. The black void was all that was seen.

"You came from the sky?" David asked.

"Yeah, I know this is kind of confusing, but I am the girl that's from the outside world."

There was no way he could ever believe me.

I continued, "I always prayed to live in this village. And it's come true."

"Ohh," David replied. "You're the girl everyone's been talking about."

"Yeah, I guess."

"So how are you enjoying life?"

"It's good. I just woke up two hours ago. But so far so good."

"Ah, that's good. Well, do you like the scenery?"

"I love it."

"Yeah, it's really great here. You'll really like it."

"I wish the real world looked like this. Then I would be truly happy."

"You'll be living here, so it won't matter much."

"What?"

"Well, I gotta go. Enjoy your time," David said, leaving in a hurry.

I saw a bench across from the tree and sat down. The park was peaceful, it was silent, and the wind blew gentle enough to put anyone to sleep. I looked at the tree, it was beautiful.

"I could live here forever," I thought. I closed my eyes and breathed in slowly. The wind caressed my cheek, and I heard the leaves rustle with every blow.

Later that afternoon, I returned to MY HOUSE. There Norah was setting the table for dinner.

"So early?" I thought.

"Hi Norah," I said, walking to her. "Do you need any help?"

"Oh, hello dear," she said, standing up. "I'm fine, I'm almost finished. How was your day?"

"It was amazing, I *REALLY* love the scenery. And everyone is so friendly."

"That's great," Norah said, laughing. "Well go ahead and get ready for supper."

"Are you sure? I really think I should help."

"No go ahead, enjoy your time here."

"Okay," I said, walking up the stairs.

Looking through the closet, I found a beautiful pink dress. On the hem were floral patterns and leaves blowing in the wind. The collar was laced with leaves. I really loved this place.

As I headed towards the stairs I could hear Norah speaking with someone.

"Well if I'm chosen, she can be my replacement. Your daughter-in-law, even," Norah whispered harshly. "Look, I know this may seem selfish, but I need to do this for myself—"

"I get that," a man interrupted her. "But what about us, and this family? We need you as much as you need us."

"I know but it's time I was finally picked."

"We all have been waiting to be picked. But if I were in the same position I would give it up to make sure you were okay."

"Well I'm sorry, but I'm going to try anyways. That's sweet of you to say you would think of me. But if that ever happened, you would have tried your hardest to leave," Norah said. Her tone was getting more and more clipped. "I want to see the other world as much as anyone else. I won the chance fair and square. End of the discussion. Now get ready, it's time for dinner."

I waited a bit to see if the conversation was over and headed down.

"Sorry I'm late," I said, walking into the dining area.

"Oh no worries," Norah said, giggling. "My husband just walked in, and my son not too long ago."

I glanced to the table and saw a man. He looked 40 and he wore a grey suit and his hair was slicked back. He had a 5 o'clock shadow. And looked similar to Mr. Gommer but cleaner.

"Hi," I said, sitting down at the table. "I'm Violet. Nice to meet you."

"Gommery," he seemed a bit annoyed. "Nice to meet you too."

He even talked like him.

Norah then called down her son. His name was Grant, he was 17. He wore a t-shirt with a clown on it. It looked like the clown from IT, and holey jeans. His hair was shaggy, and he was really dazed.

We finished our evening meal and headed to bed.

I lay there and heard voices. It was my mother. I got up and looked out the window. I saw her, my father, and a man.

"How could this have happened?" She was crying. "Why hasn't she woken up?"

My father held her.

"I don't know. She seems to be in a coma. I will have to look into this later," the man left, the door slammed behind him.

"Why? Why?" my mother asked. "What could have done this?"

"I don't know. It's going to be okay. She'll wake up. We just have to pray."

She looked at the ornament.

"This happened because of this stupid ornament!" She reached for it, but my father grabbed her arm.

"Don't, this can probably be the key to waking her."

"Okay," she whispered.

They left the room.

I was asleep? That couldn't have been right. Maybe my soul was gone? But I felt myself. It was all too much to take in. And if what David said was true, that I would stay there forever, then my mother would be pained forever also. It was too much to take in, in one day, so I turned in for the night.

In the morning I returned to Transformation Park. I figured I could probably find David again. As I sat down, a man walked up.

"Hello, Violet," he said. He was tall, more than the average tall person. He had a mustache, it was thick and had the perfect curl. He wore a suit and a top hat. It made me giggle.

"I see everything is good. And you are happy?"

"Yes. Um if I may be so bold. What is your name?"

"Ah, yes. Excuse me. My name is Joe Jon Jones," wow quite the name. "I am the mayor of Autumn."

"Autumn? Is that the name of this town?"

"Yes."

"I love it."

"Of course! This town is for you. It is what you want it to be."

"Wow, I never knew this town was created with my ideals."

"Well, it wasn't created by you. It just conformed to your thoughts, to make you happy."

"Oh," that didn't make sense, so I continued on. "There is another question mayor. How am I here and home at the same time?"

"Your soul and mind are here. You are like a seed. your body is dormant, for now."

"So, when I want to leave I can go back to my body?"

"Oh no. No no no. You cannot leave. Once you are here, you're here."

"Well then how will my body last?"

"Someone from the village will take your place. I guess since it's your body, I can tell you the candidates. You can even choose who's best," Joe Jon Jones said. "There is Norah, since you stay at her place, she is the first choice. There is David, who I heard you have met already. And there is Joanne

Jon Jones, my wife who you will soon meet."

What? How could this have happened? Why? I just wanted to live in this town I watched for years. Suddenly, I heard the ring of the clock outside. It was midnight. The leaves on the tree lit up, the colors were mystical, and glistened. Everyone gathered around me. The three of them, Norah, David, and Joanne stood in front of me.

"Let the ceremony commence!" Joe Jon Jones announced. Everyone screamed and cheered.

"Now Miss Violet, choose the candidate you like," Joe Jon Jones continued. "Hurry now. We don't have much time."

"No. No, I can't. I don't want to be here, I wanna go home!"

"Now now Miss Violet, you know the rules. Choose someone or we'll choose for you."

"No, I won't!"

"NOW! Choose NOW!"

"NO!"

"Fine! Have it your way."

Joe Jon Jones waved a hand and a man came with a box. Joe Jon Jones reached inside and took out a folded paper.

"David!" Joe Jon Jones screamed.

The crowd erupted into cheers. I looked at David and he smiled. The villagers crowded him. He looked back at me and mouthed, "*Sucks to be you.*"

Everything shook. I looked to the sky and saw my father was carrying the ornament to my room.

"Maybe this will wake her up. If she hears the sound of the music," my father said. He sat the ornament near my head.

The tree illuminated everything, and David disappeared. I looked at myself to see if this was real. He got up, and looked at the ornament, my eyes were green. His eyes were gentle as he smiled,

"I love this ornament."

CHAPTER EIGHT
THE MIRRORS

Some say when you're dead you can watch your own funeral. In my case it's a little true. But I'm jumping the gun. I should tell you how I died first.

It wasn't that horrible or tragic of a death, it was, how can I put it, boring. I suffered from a pretty weak heart. Even just the slightest excitement or lack of sleep could stop my heart. However, the ironic part was that I had a very active family. In the winter they snowboarded, in the summer they surfed. Climbed mountains, sky dived, scuba dived, anything possible.

So, I'll start the day before my death. My parents were really psyched about going bungee jumping and they needed to find a babysitter for my brother and me. My mom sat on the computer, and my dad read want ads in the paper.

They were really stressed out they couldn't find anyone that could do it on such short notice.

"Mom, dad. you don't need to worry about us. I can babysit Matt, or I can stay home, and you bring him with."

I really wanted to stay home by myself, I *rarely* got any peace with them.

"I don't know if that's such a good idea," my mom said. "You know the doctor said that you shouldn't be left alone for a long time. Anything can happen."

"I agree with your mother," dad said, being as useless in a conversation as ever.

"But I'm almost 16. I can take care of myself. I know not to do anything strenuous or stay up too late. I'll be fine," I know I wasn't thinking very maturely, but I needed alone time.

I continued, "Besides, I'm pretty sure Matt would love to go bungee jumping or at least see it."

"Well," my mother paused. "Okay, you are very mature for your age. I think you'll be fine."

"Thank you," I said, hugging her tightly. "I'm heading to bed. You guys should also get some sleep. It's not safe to drive when you're tired. Night."

"Don't worry about us, night hun," dad said, still reading want ads.

That night, I dreamt I was looking in a mirror. I stood there, just brushing my hair. The light kept flickering. A shadow or dark figure about 6'0" stood behind me in the tub. Its eyes were red, it stood there, a red sliver of a smile on its face. It held that creepy smile while I stood there brushing. After a while I finally finished. As I took the hair out of the brush and tossed it in the garbage, the smile on the thing disappeared. It frowned, I open the cabinet and put the brush away. Its eyes lowered, a menacing look on its face. I watched it through the mirror never turning around. It was mad, I walked towards the door, its head followed my every movement, suddenly, the thing came at me in a flash and I was jarred awake.

I leaned over the edge of my bed, trying to catch my breath and lower my heart rate. This was the first time I could be home by myself, I wasn't going to let it be ruined. Not by anything. So I figured it would be best to not tell mom. I eventually calmed down and turned to face the wall.

"She can't know this happened."

The day of my death wasn't that bad. Just like any other day, whoever said, the day you die is fun and peaceful, was probably crazy or high when they died. In the morning my parents, brother, and I ate breakfast. I turned on the TV like usual to check the weather.

"Hey, they're saying there's supposed to be a bad storm today. You guys sure you don't want to postpone leaving for a day?"

"Nah, we'll be fine," dad said, not even looking up from his book. "If we wait, we'll be off track and might miss our time."

"I guess, just be careful."

"You're such a worrywart, it'll be okay," mom said, kissing my forehead.

My family didn't care about safety. Their logic was *whatever happens, happens*. It was quite annoying. But I guess if they were worried about safety they wouldn't be doing such psychotic activities or letting me stay by myself for the weekend.

"Well," dad said, and sat down his silverware. "We better hit the road if we want to beat this storm."

He winked and got up.

"Have fun," I said, seeing them off.

I watched as they drove away before heading to the living room. It was by far the quietest the house had been since forever. I sighed and grabbed a book, plopped on the couch and readed. I had to have read for about 4 hours. I got up to make some lunch, halfway through the door, out of nowhere one of the mirrors in the living room fell and shattered. Pieces were all over.

"Great," I thought. *"I was off to a lovely start. Mom's not going to believe me when I tell her it fell by itself."*

As I cleaned up the shards, I saw something black in the reflection and looked up to see nothing. I picked up most of the shards but cut my finger on a tiny piece and headed to the bathroom to clean the cut. While rinsing I saw a black figure in the window and looked back quickly. No one.

"That dreams got you all sorts of messed up girl." I shook my head and headed towards the kitchen. I made delicious sautéed vegetables and some of the cake mom left for me to snack on.

At about 4 pm I could hear the rain on the roof. *So, the storms finally coming,* I thought, pulling the covers from the back of the couch. Suddenly, a huge bolt of lightning hit outside of the living room window and shattered it. It startled me so much, I had a heart attack and I died. Lame right? Were you expecting some kind of climax horror movie death? Sorry, it wasn't as climatic as I made it seem.

And like that I was dead, such a lame way to go. My dead lifeless body just lay there for about a day before my mom's friend stopped over to check on me. But after a day it's too late. I think your organs start to fail and you got like 5 minutes to harvest the organs before they're useless. I don't know. I picked that up from Grey's Anatomy when the guy chose to die and donate his organs. But back to the point, I can continue telling my story to you.

What happened next? I was at my own wake. I saw my mother crying, and my dad comforting her. I never thought such a colorful room would be filled with such darkness. I wanted to tell my mom, "It's okay, it's not her fault I'm dead."

She kept saying since they got back this was all her fault. My little brother cried in my grandparents' arms.

Who knew they would be so upset over this. I felt bad. I wanted to tell them, "It's okay, that I was there." But after I left my body, I sat there freaking out for a bit, after a while I was sucked inside of the mirror over the fireplace. I've been here ever since. I read online that it was a superstition, but people in the Victorian era and some religions believed that you have to cover the mirrors in a room where a person has died. In the Victorian belief, you have to cover the mirrors because the soul of the person will be stuck in the mirror forever, and something about the devil. But I didn't believe in it. I guess the superstition was true. I tried everything to get out of here.

I keep getting off track.

I watched my family mourn for another hour before heading to the church for burial. After everyone left, it was silent. I felt even lonelier than ever. I wondered if this was supposed to be my afterlife. Stuck in a mirror, watching my family forever, or until Matt breaks this mirror. My eyes glanced across the room. That room was amazing. I guess when you're dead you appreciate life more. I looked at the couch then the bookshelf, fireplace, carpet, the pastel flower wallpaper, wooden floors. I couldn't complain if this was going to be it. In a way it was serene, nostalgic. I continued to look around the room. I looked at the millions of mirrors my mom had. I looked in each one, when I looked at the one in front of me, I could see there were infinite mirror reflections. It looked like a path leading somewhere. I looked intensely as far into the path as I could. Inside, I saw a figure. It peeked from a corner and disappeared again.

"Weird," I thought. *"Must be my spirit eyes playing tricks on me."*

I wanted to see how far it could go on before something changed. Again, the figure appeared, except it went onto the path and ran toward me. Nothing could have been scarier than that. I couldn't move. I was scared. I didn't even know how to move, dead or in a mirror. My breathing got heavier as it came closer.

"It's at the other mirror," I reassured myself. *"No way can it get me from here."*

As it got closer I remembered where I saw it. It was from my dream! It stood behind me, watching me brush my hair. As it became clearer to see, I saw it had the same look on its "face." It's red eyes looked at me, it wasn't smiling like before. I didn't even see a mouth. Its arms were out.

"Please don't come any closer," I whispered. "I don't know what you want from me, please go away."

It came to a stop. It stood there, its eyes were piercing and frightening. It smiled its creepy smile and grabbed my shoulders. I closed my eyes as it tugged me backwards, a breath escaped my mouth.

"Shit!" I thought. *"This is a mirror! It's reflecting my side too!"*

I felt the wind blowing through my hair and brushing my cheeks. I opened my eyes to see infinite reflections zoom past. It was like a horrible rollercoaster ride that went backwards, surrounded by multiple optical illusions. I couldn't help but tremble at what was happening. It kept the same smile on its face as it went back. It seemed like we were going for miles until it turned a corner. We were in a bathroom, my bathroom. It opened the cabinet and took out my brush and slid what I assumed was its hand out to give to me.

"What," I managed to stutter. "You want me to brush my hair?"

It nodded its head and went into the tub. Its gaze was intense, just like in my dream, it watched as I kept brushing.

60 years had passed, all I did was brush my hair. Every day and night, every hour, minute, second, I brushed my hair. And it watched a look of delight and content on its face as it stood there in the tub. I brushed my hair, for all of eternity.

CHAPTER NINE
THE NEW HOUSE

Hazel was 14, she was the age where most teenagers spent their time on their phones or had attitudes towards their parents. There was never a day when her parents didn't anger her. Many days she spent loathing the sight of her mother as she cooked dinner or disgust towards her stepfather. Every night, she thought about her opportunity to escape. She couldn't wait to move out of there. Hazel didn't always have a problem with her parents.

Maybe it was when her father died. She was 10 and her mother, Diane remarried within a year. Her mother worried she couldn't support her children financially and figured marrying the next guy would be best.

Before her mother remarried, before her father passed, Hazel was happy. Her and her father were closer than anything. They would camp in the woods on a Tuesday, or ditch school and work to play lazertag. Her time with him was amazing.

The man her mother married was Randy Connor. A quiet guy, every day he worked in his shed, he never talked, never smiled, just worked. During supper he would quietly eat and return to his shed. He wasn't always like that. For the first 2 years of their marriage he was warm, quiet but attentive, and that was why Hazel's mother felt he was perfect. But as their 3rd year rolled along, he became reserved, and very unaffectionate. Hazel knew something was up. At night she locked her door, worried about what he might do. He was crazy, that much she knew.

Hazel looked out the window at the passing landscape. There wasn't a phone reception but at least she had her music. Her parents decided it was best to move. With her mother's work being moved to Roxbury, New Hampshire, it would be easier than to commute from Sullivan. It was originally her late father's idea for them to move to Roxbury, they always wanted to own a little café in an area with very few people.

Hazel and her younger brother James disagreed with their move to such a remote location. They would be leaving behind their friends, and their school. and for Hazel the love of her—high school—life, Andrew.

James sat on the other side of the car, playing Minecraft, like usual. Moping about not seeing his best friend Timmy again.

The drive was short but felt like an eternity to Hazel. When they arrived, Hazel and James were shocked at the sight of their new home. Hazel looked up and down at the exterior of the house. The house was 3 stories. The paint was worn out, and the wood could be seen. The windows on the second floor were broken, and nothing but trees surrounded their home.

"You've got to be kidding me," Hazel said, closing the car door.

"It's fine," Diane said. "It may not be a beautiful country home, but it definitely is a keeper."

"And how much did you pay for this house?" Hazel asked.

"It was on sale," Diane responded. "The house hasn't been able to sell. Not to mention the value for it has gone down. A lucky find."

"Well, looking at it now, it's no wonder people didn't want it," Hazel rolled her eyes and walked to the house.

When Hazel entered, she felt someone staring at her. Chills ran down her spine and she glanced around, no one.

"Weird," she thought.

Hazel opened the door and yelled to her mom who struggled to carry in three boxes, "Mom, can I choose any room?"

"Go ahead hun," Diane said, as everything in her arms tumbled out.

"Klutz," Hazel scoffed slamming the door.

Hazel walked to the third floor, there were four rooms, three of them were closed. She looked at the fourth door, shrugged, and walked inside.

"Guess it was meant to be," Hazel said.

When Hazel entered, she first noticed the wallpaper. Pink bunnies were placed randomly on a bright strawberry pink wallpaper. Hazel rolled her eyes.

She continued to look across the room, there was furniture placed inside. Her eyes glanced from the window to the cream nightstand by her bed. Her bedding was light pink with sleeping pink dust bunnies.

"Could this room be anymore girly," Hazel said, cynically.

She looked at the cream dresser, on top was a small mirror and a beautiful snow globe. She was mesmerized, inside was a fairy sitting atop a rock. She looked sad, hunched over she cradled herself. Hazel turned the nob, and a soothing familiar song played. She couldn't place where it came from, but she knew she would keep the globe.

Hazel sighed before saying, "I guess this room isn't all that bad."

Hazel felt the same eyes watching her and turned to the door. No one. Hazel slowly walked to the door and closed it. Her eyes went back to the snow globe, she couldn't shake the thought she knew it.

Later that evening Hazel rested in bed reading when she heard a knock at her door.

"Come in," she said.

No answer.

"Come in," she yelled louder.

Still no answer.

Hazel growled as she got up and swung the door open full force.

"WHAT?" she screamed.

No one was there. Hazel was furious and stormed to James' room.

"Next time you want to annoy someone, why don't you drop dead first," Hazel snapped, leaving his doorway.

"I didn't even do anything," James hollered back.

"Annoying bastard," Hazel mumbled. "I really do wish he'd drop dead. It'd do us all a favor."

Hazel plopped on her bed and looked at the ceiling. Looking very closely she noticed a pair of eyes drawn above her bed.

"That's so creepy," she thought. "No wonder I was getting chills."

Hazel yawned and dozed off.

She woke to a strong force as if being pushed off the bed. Startled, Hazel took deep breaths to calm her racing heart. She glanced frantically across the room nothing was there, but she felt someone's gaze nearby. She looked up at the ceiling. The eyes stared fiercely at her, as if glaring into her soul.

"Mom," she screamed.

Diane ran into the room, "What's wrong?"

"I feel like someone's messing with me. Someone's always staring at me," Hazel cried. "Someone pushed me."

"Honey calm down. There's nothing here. I promise."

"Well promises won't save my life!"

"Hazel, if you're that scared, go sleep on the floor in James' room."

"No thanks," Hazel said, with disgust. "I'd rather be kidnapped by that person."

"Okay, that's your problem. Goodnight."

Hazel was left alone, "That's right, anything is better than being with him."

The rest of the night was peaceful. In the morning Hazel asked Randy to paint over the eyes in her room. He looked at her strangely.

"What eyes?"

Hazel slowly said, "There are eyes painted over my bed."

"Well, I'll get on it right away."

"Alright."

Hazel watched as Randy painted over the eyes. As the left eye disappeared a sense of dread and foreboding washed over her. The room grew colder and Hazel began to feel faint.

"Are you okay?" Randy asked.

"Yeah, I think the fumes from the paint are getting to me."

"Right, just rest up downstairs or outside."

As they left the room, Hazel heard a whisper, "Don't go."

She turned around before carefully walking out of her room. Once they reached the first floor, Hazel decided to go for a walk. Their house was surrounded by woods, so she figured she might see a deer or two walking around. She walked along the fence until she found a tiny opening. Hazel crouched down to see what was on the other side. Through the hole, Hazel saw a faint glimmer before it disappeared. She could hear the sound of light footsteps. A tiny foot came across the hole. Hazel could hear the sound of cooing, it sounded very cute. Hazel couldn't help but giggle. As if it heard her, the tiny creature became quiet. It stayed in place, then the creature began to crouch. Slowly, Hazel saw its knee, then the other. One hand after the other, until suddenly,

"Hazel," Diane shouted. "It's time for lunch!"

With that, the tiny fella ran away.

"Damnit Diane," Hazel snarled and headed indoors.

"How was your walk?" Diane said.

"I wouldn't know considering it was ruined before I could even leave the yard," Hazel said in a snippy tone.

"I'm sorry, you were gone for 20 minutes, so I figured you would have come back."

"20 minutes? I was gone for 2."

"No, honey. You were gone way longer than that. Look at the time."

"Someone had a lot of fun walking in nature," snickered James.

"Yeah, something you wouldn't know about," Hazel remarked.

"Now calm down you two and eat your meal," interrupted Diane.

"Whatever," Hazel responded.

After lunch, Hazel went back to the spot in the fence, but nothing was there.

Confused, Hazel said, "What? I'm pretty sure this was the spot."

Hazel searched the fence. Nothing. Disappointed, she returned to her room.

"Great the one time I find something interesting, it's ruined." Hazel dove onto her bed. "Guess I'll never be happy again."

"Yes, you will," a voice said, it came from the corner of the room. "Don't give up you can find happiness. And soon!"

"Who's there?" Hazel shot up from the bed and looked around. Nothing was there. "Come out, right now."

"Wow, you've become such a snippy person," the voice said. "You don't even recognize me?"

Hazel looked confused, how could she remember someone she couldn't even see?

The voice continued, "I remember when we used to eat ice cream straight from the tub, and how your mother would get angry."

It chuckled, and next to Hazel a spot on the bed sunk in. Instinctively, Hazel tried to dart for the door.

"Don't run, you have nothing to be afraid of," the voice said, as a strong force grabbed her arm. "It's me, papa."

"Bullshit, he's dead. Do you really think I would fall for the cliché 'oh your dead father has come back to make you happy again,' plot? Not this girl," Hazel tried to pull away, but it was too strong. "Let go. I know you're some ghoul trying to eat me. It's not going to work, so stop trying."

The voice erupted in loud laughter, "That's my girl, smart as could be. I raised you well. But seriously it's me."

"Then why can't I see you?"

"Because I don't have a physical form. The only way for you to actually see me is..." the voice paused. "You don't believe me, no point in continuing."

"Wait, go on, I'll listen first before making any decisions."

"Atta girl, the only way to actually see me, is for you to find something that was my possession. With that you'll have to conduct a tiny ceremony and voila! I'm back in this world."

"I don't know, the real dad wouldn't put me in this kind of a situation. What happens if you're not him, huh?"

"I eat you and your whole family, or maybe just your family and keep you for company. I mean that's the worst that could happen, my body can't stay too long in the living world. So, it wouldn't be all that bad.

Just survive long enough until my body disappears."

"You're honest," Hazel said, skeptical.

"Of course, I'm your father. I said I would never lie to you and I meant it. Now what do you say? Can you give your old pops another chance at life?"

Hazel hesitated, was this really her dad? Could she really be able to spend time with him and get things back to the way they used to be?

Hazel sighed, she knew this would be a bad idea, but she agreed.

"Really?! I love you," her father said. Hazel felt an intense force wrap itself around her.

"Are you trying to hug me?"

"Yeah."

"Well, it's not working."

"I know..."

"I'll be right back," Hazel ran out of the room. "Wait, what else do I have to get?"

"Bring chalk, 5 candles, matches or a lighter, boil vinegar with a eucalyptus, eye of newt, a few drops of blood from those related. Basically, you or James. And a fresh corpse."

"A corpse?"

"Just kidding, I wouldn't do that to you. Temporary times are good enough for now."

"Right," Hazel slowly said, as she left.

"Oh, and don't tell anyone. Not that they would believe you anyway."

"I don't think we have vinegar, would salt work?"

"No," he yelled nervously. "Salt and vinegar are not the same. Besides, I'm allergic. You know that."

"Uh, no I didn't"

"Oh well, run along."

Hazel reached the kitchen, it was to her and her father's luck Diane just bought eucalyptus plants for decoration, she looked up what eye of newt was and boiled the ingredients. After it was finished, she returned to her room.

"Are you still here?"

"Of course, hunny bunch," her father said. "Are you ready?"

"Yeah."

"Great, first things first. Use the chalk to draw as perfect a circle as you can, in the inside draw a diamond shape with points on each line. Place a candle on each point of the diamond and one in the middle. Then pour the liquid around the circle. Not all of it but some. Here are the words you have to say."

Hazel did as she was told.

"Stand back," he said. "Don't want you to be a sacrifice ha-ha."

Hazel chuckled uncomfortably.

"Why haven't you started yet?"

"You didn't say anything."

"I nodded...oh."

"Yeah."

Hazel took a deep breath. Her heart was racing. Was this a good idea? What if he really wasn't him? But if this chance was real, she could finally have him back. It was a risk. And a clear chance, if he wasn't, he'd eat her family.

Hazel took a long deep inhale, as she exhaled, she chanted the words, "Efil ot emoc, Irum, parl, karrum. Uoy ot semoc efil yam, barro."

As she chanted, a bright light swelled up from a tiny point and covered the circle. A gust of wind filled the room causing Hazel to fly onto the bed. In an instant, the bright light flashed, and everything went dark. Hazel opened her eyes to see a man hunched in the circle. He was wearing clothing, clothing similar to what her father wore before he died. Hazel got up and cautiously walked to him.

"Dad?" She asked.

The man sluggishly breathed as if tired.

"You alright?"

The man stood up and turned to Hazel.

"Thanks a lot kiddo."

Hazel looked with pure delight, her father was back.

"Papa," Hazel squealed jumping into his arms.

"It's nice to see you too," he chuckled.

"Do you know how much I missed you? And how ruined the family is?"

"Yes, I know it all, I'm sorry I left."

"Good, now you and mom can get back together and bye bye Randy, lets go," Hazel turned to open the door when her father grabbed her arm.

"No, you can't tell ANYONE I'm here," his eyes were ferocious. "If you do, I'll disappear."

"Okay," she responded faintly.

"Good, now shall we have some fun?" he said, with a mischievous grin.

"What do you have in mind?"

"Oh, I don't know, maybe pull pranks on Randy and James?"

"Let's do it!"

For the rest of the day Hazel and her father pulled mean tricks on her family. They couldn't figure out who it was, because Hazel was always in her room. Her family was getting frustrated, sad, and hurt by their strange experiences. And Hazel loved it, this was her revenge for what they were doing to her.

"So how do you like your room? I specifically had it designed like this," he said, with a proud look.

"*You* made it like this," she emphasized. "Don't you think it's a little...to babyish and girly."

"But you liked girly, did you really change all that much in 4 years?"

"I mean, I guess not. It's not that bad, just threw me off with the huge burst of pink."

He chuckled, "Sorry about that. Man, you don't know how long I've waited to give you this."

"How long?"

"Years, before you were even born. Your mother and I set sight on this place long ago. I bought the house but because of our work we had to stay in Sullivan. But even though I died before the move, I'm glad to see you in this room."

"That's good..." Hazel didn't know how to respond. She had this feeling something was off. But it was her father, what could he do to harm her and why would he?

"You should head to bed, we have a lot more to do in the morning," he said, with a wink.

And with that, Hazel's bad hunch disappeared, "Okay, goodnight."

Later that evening, Hazel woke to a weird sound. It was her father laughing silently in the corner. A tiny blue light illuminated his face.

"Dad?" Hazel got up, "What are you doing? Don't you sleep?"

"Sleep is for the living."

"Right," she mumbled. "What's that light?"

"This? Nothing, don't worry about it," then he whispered, "Just planning to have a little fun."

"What'd you say?"

"Nothing, don't worry."

Hazel stared at him his back still turned towards her. Then a spark went off, "Hey, I was also wondering where you got this snow globe? It's beautiful."

"Snow globe?" He responded getting up, the light behind his back. "What snow globe?"

"There," she pointed.

"I don't see it. There's nothing on your dresser."

"Could he really not see it?" she thought.

"Never mind," she said. "I was just messing with you."

"Ha. Ha. Ha. Don't joke around with this old man," he got closer. He whispered, "Playing tricks on a ghost isn't such a bright idea."

Stunned, Hazel stood in place.

"I'm just pulling your leg. Just remember, life lesson, don't pull any pranks on your ally."

"I won't, not anymore."

"Great, now go to sleep."

In the morning Hazel woke to Diane and Randy arguing. Her father stood in the doorway laughing.

"What's going on?" Hazel asked groggy.

"I pranked your mother and Randy. They're sure to break up after what I did."

"What *DID* you do?"

"Go see for yourself," he smiled moving from the door.

Hazel rushed into her parents' room, and her mouth dropped. She let out a gasp, "What happened?!"

Both Diane and Randy became quiet and looked at Hazel. Hazel looked around the room. It was completely trashed. Lamps and glasses were broken, their bedding torn, their love seat shredded, and saw dust was poured all over their room.

"Please Hazel, let your mother and me speak," Randy asked.

"Go to your room, or outside," Diane ordered.

Hazel rushed back to her room, "Why the hell would you do that?"

"Watch your language," he barked. "It's a joke, besides you're the one begging they split. Now you don't want that?"

"Not the way you're doing it."

"How ungrateful, they'll get over it soon," he retorted. "So, what's our plan for today?"

"Nothing," Hazel said. "*I'm* going for a walk. If you want to come with you can."

"I can't go outside."

"Well I'll see you when I get back."

Hazel walked out the room and out the house. As she walked in her yard she glanced at her window. She could see her father watching her.

"If this isn't getting creepy, I don't know what is," she thought.

She walked along the fence and saw the same tiny hole. She crouched down to see there was a tiny back resting on the fence.

"Hello," she said, gently to ensure it wouldn't get scared.

The creature jumped back and stared at the giant in its space. The creature was pale, it wore glasses, and freckles ran across its nose. It looked like a fairy.

"She can see me," it said, with a strong English accent.

"It's okay, don't be frightened. I won't hurt you."

"Oh no, what ta do, what ta do. I'll be in big trouble," he said, running in circles. "I got it! I'll...no no no, that's no good. I could...no but that'll get me in trouble. Maybe I can say I was neva here. She can't fit anyway."

Hazel watched the creature mumble to itself. Until it quickly faced her, "What should I do? You're not su'posed to see me. I'm gonna be in big trouble."

"Well, I can walk away, and we can never speak of this again. That way no one knows I saw you."

"That's a good idea. I walk away, neva speak of again. Right, that works. Goodbye."

"Bye," Hazel said, as the tiny creature scurried off.

Hazel was curious, but her judgement told her not to look. She got up and saw her father still staring at her from a crack in the curtains. She walked to the back of the yard, away from her father's intense gaze.

"Now for some peace and quiet," she leaned on the biggest tree in the yard.

As much as she hated being there, the scenery wasn't all bad. It was actually, very soothing. She could hear leaves blowing with the wind. And a warm summer breeze caressed her cheeks and she dozed off. She woke to Diane calling her name. She sounded angry. Hazel rushed in the house, praying it wasn't her father's doing again.

"What is it mom?"

"Did you do this?" Diane pointed to James' game.

"No, why would I? I was outside this whole time. I literally just woke up."

"And you expect me to believe that how?"

"You can even ask Randy. He saw me leave the house."

"Well Randy's not here, so we'll go with what we think."

"But why would I? Seriously. I would never break his stuff."

"Well you were really mad at me yesterday. You thought I was messing with you and told me to drop dead," James responded timidly.

"But I knew that wasn't you, I realized that—" she paused. "I was just hearing things."

"Go to your room Hazel. You'll be there for the rest of the day."

"Oh my god, why do I bother."

Hazel stormed up to her room, "Why would you break his games?"

"Well you wished he would die, and I can't kill my own son, so I did the next best thing. Broke his games."

"Yeah, but you got me in trouble in the process."

"And? That just means we can hang out together even longer."

"Seriously? You think I'd want to hang around with you after this?"

Hazel left the room.

"You can't leave. Your mother told you to stay here," her father said, following her.

"I thought you said you couldn't leave the room."

"No, I can't leave the house. How do you think I did all those pranks? With my 'ghostly powers.' HA!"

As he laughed Randy came up the stairs. Instinctively Hazel looked back at her dad, who put his finger to his mouth.

"Don't say anything. Only you can see and hear me."

"Who were you talking to?" Randy asked.

"No one, I was just repeating something from a show I just finished."

"Alright," he looked suspicious. "I could have sworn I saw something just now, coming up the stairs, but it might just be me getting old."

"Ha-ha maybe," Hazel laughed.

"Didn't your mother send you to your room?"

"Yeah, but I was going to apologize for it, even though I didn't do it."

"I know, I believe you. So, I told your mother I saw you sleeping on the tree outback. Told her, they might have broken in the box. A lot of weird stuff has been happening since we moved here," he remarked staring passed her, then looking left then right. "That's why I'm up here, to grant you your freedom."

"Thanks," she said, hugging him. "You're a life saver."

"Literally and figuratively," he said, with a serious tone. He placed his arm around her and said, "Now let's go downstairs and have some fun."

Hazel's father who watched their encounter whispered to Hazel, "Something about this guy doesn't seem right. Watch out for him, it could be my father senses or something else, just be careful."

"You probably get the wrong impression because he undoes what you do," she thought.

For the first time in forever Hazel had fun with her family. She even apologized that James' games were broken and for saying he should drop dead. She didn't hear a peep from her father. She said goodnight and went to her room.

Sitting seriously on her bed, her father looked at Hazel and motioned for her to sit next to him. Something was off, and Hazel trembled. She could leave, or she could trust him. She took a deep breath and sat next to him.

"You look more serious now than you have since you got a body."

"Yes well, my body will disappear tomorrow, so I won't be able to hang out with my favorite child any longer. I'm a little down in the dumps is all."

Hazel was glad, and a bit sad, "That's too bad. If only there were a way to help you stay longer."

"There is, I'm just a little confused about why my body only lasted a few days. I should have lasted a month at least. Did you use all the ingredients? Eucalyptus, eye of newt, and a few drops of your blood?"

"Oh, I forgot the blood."

"No wonder, we'll just have to keep applying the liquid daily."

"I poured it out."

"Seriously?"

"You didn't say we needed it after, and it smelled. So, I dumped it. If it means anything, I can just boil some more."

"No, that won't do. It has to be the same one used to summon me. Guess tonight will be our last time together...unless," he hesitated. "Never mind I wouldn't do that to you."

"Do what?"

"It's nothing, really."

"You can't start saying something and not finish it. You know I hate that."

"Sorry," he chuckled. "The other option, would be for you to come with me."

"What?! You want me to die!?"

"You wouldn't be dead, you would just cross over with me. You know, you'll be a human living in the land of the dead."

"I don't know if I can do that."

"You love me, don't you?"

"I do, but—"

"Then you can prove it by coming with me. You're my precious daughter. I can't leave this world without you. The other side is lonely."

"Look, I love you, but I don't know if I can just leave the living world. I haven't even lived my life yet."

"But you always wanted to escape this family. Ever since I died, you weren't happy. You can be happy with me on the other side. Death will be perceived as whatever you want it to be."

"You're going to have to give me time on this."

"I understand, we will talk again in an hour. That should be enough time."

"Right, well I'll think somewhere else. *Alone.*"

Hazel left the room, before returning. She walked over with a large piece of cardboard and placed it in front of the window. And closed the curtains.

"Why'd you do that?" he asked.

"Because I don't need you watching every move I make."

"Alright."

Hazel left the room and headed to the first floor. While passing the second, Hazel saw Randy working in one of the rooms. He was fixing the window and repainting the walls.

"Hey, I'm going outside. I need some fresh air."

"Just stay in the yard."

Hazel scoffed, as if a 14-year-old would get kidnapped in a secluded wooded area. She went outside and walked along the fence. A tiny light shined in one spot and Hazel went over. It was the same hole the tiny fairy was in. She bent down to see what was inside. It was livelier than ever. Tiny feet passed the hole, and she could hear the sound of a city. It was the cutest thing for Hazel. A little city of fairies. Hazel giggled, and a book dropped on the ground.

"You again," the voice said. "I thought you would forget about this place. It was a deal."

"Well no, I said, we should forget we met. And you aren't doing a good job of that."

"Well why are you here?" the fairy said.

"I needed fresh air, I'm in quite the dilemma," she snickered. "My dead father came out of nowhere. I gave him a body and now he wants me to cross over to the other side with him."

"Oh, that's bad. Very bad, very bad indeed. I will tell my masta what is happening. Wait here. Wait here," the fairy said, fidgeting away.

"Alright, I'll just lay here…"

Five minutes later, the fairy came back, along with it were bigger feet.

"Right here masta, the human girl is right here."

The hole expanded wider to where what looked like the queen could be seen.

"Hello," she said. "It seems like you're in a bit of a predicament."

"Yeah, dead father comes back to life, pulls a bunch of pranks on my family, wants me to go to the world of the dead with him, you know, the usual."

She chuckled, "Well, I wouldn't call it the usual, but we can certainly help."

"Really?! Please do!"

"Don't worry, one of our own is already helping."

"I didn't see him leave."

"Because he was never here."

"Right. Well I should probably tell him no."

"Yes, that's a good idea. And if anything happens, our person will come to help."

Hazel steadied her breathing as she walked up the stairs and into her room.

"The answer is no," she managed to say.

"Well, hello to you too," he said, sitting down a book. "You must be so confused on what to do. My question was will you go with me, not do you want to stay here."

"My answer is no to going with you."

Her father was stunned, "What do you mean no? I'm your father, you can't abandon me. I didn't abandon you when you were in need."

"Yeah, you did, you died."

"And that could be helped how?"

"It can't be, and that's why it's not fair," she stayed not too far from the door fearing what he would do. "Just because you died doesn't mean you can take away my life too. I suffered when you died, but I adapted to that change. And you have to adapt to yours."

Her father stood silently. His fists were clenched, she could see the veins in his arms as he tightened them harder. He was pissed, and there was no telling what he would do.

"And you call yourself my daughter," he said, his teeth clinched together. "I should have known James would have been the better child. I wasted so many years on someone ungrateful. I helped you! Yet you won't even do this one thing for me?"

"Look I'm sorry, I didn't mean to hurt you. I just want to live," she quivered. Hazel was slowly walking backwards to the door. "I love you papa, but I can't die. Not yet."

"It's too late for that," he said, as he lunged towards her.

Hazel dodged to the right, slamming into her drawer. The snow globe fell and landed on Hazel. Her father attacked with full speed but was repelled by a light.

"Argh," he groaned. He looked all around her but saw nothing.

"He can't see the snow globe," Hazel thought. "This is my chance to run."

Hazel grabbed the snow globe and ran past him.

She bumped into Randy, "What's going on? Are you okay?

"I'm fine, please hurry inside your room."

"Let me guess, your 'father' showed his true colors finally?"

"Wait, you knew."

"Of course. I knew he was the one pranking us, messing up our room, and breaking James' games. I knew he was there the whole time."

"I'm sorry, I just wanted to see him again, but now he wants me to go to the other side with him. I said no, and now he's trying to kill me. The only thing protecting me is this snow globe."

"And the mirror."

"The mirror?"

"Yes, both the mirror and snow globe were there to protect you."

"That's right, he couldn't see them when I asked about them. But how did you know?"

"I placed them there," he said, instantly. "When your mother showed me this place, I saw your father in the window. That's how I knew. And painted over those eyes."

As he finished, they heard a large crackle and her father yelled.

"What happened to him?"

"Salt, it keeps ghosts from entering or leaving certain places."

"You piece of shit," her father yelled. "I should have finished you from the start!"

"As if you could," Randy snorted. "Hazel stand back, the salt won't act for long."

Hazel glanced at the ground, the salt was burning and dissipating. Hazel cowered behind Randy as he pulled out a strange object.

"Ecalp siht evael, detnaw ton era uoy. I banish you to the realm between life and death for all eternity. No evom, no evom no evom won!"

Hazel's father screamed in agony as he chanted.

In a monstrous voice he said, "You'll regret this."

And as he disappeared, his form turned to what looked like a goblin, or some type of gremlin. All that was left was a scorch mark and the smell of burned flesh.

"I should have known. I'm so stupid. I guess that wasn't my father the whole time?"

"No, it was. Your father was a Markshnier."

"A...Markshnier?"

"They're a type of goblin that lives in the human world. They aren't dangerous creatures, but they will at times lose control and eat a human, or cause havoc. They don't live very long and usually have roughly 2-3 offspring, one or two to stay in the human world to create more and one to take back with them to the other side. Though your father made the mistake of marrying and mating with a human. Human blood is stronger than most goblin species and a few monsters. When he died, your mother had his body cremated, so there was nothing left for his spirit to return to. He then fled to this house which he planned on taking you in. All he needed was a body."

"But why did he latch on to me?"

"They stick to one child, and bond with them so the child is conflicted with leaving them. Maybe because he felt your blood was stronger than James' or because you were his first born, he chose you."

"That explains why he wanted to use my blood to help create his body."

"Which obviously would never have worked considering your blood was contaminated with a human's. It would have to be a pureblood for it to work successfully."

"Does mom know?"

"A little, she had her suspicions something was wrong with him, but she never knew what."

"Are you a Markshnier too?"

"Oh, heavens no, I would never be such a lowly specie," he sneered. "I'm what you would call a fairy. Or rather a sub-specie of fairies. I'm a huemonary, the biggest sub-species. The tiny people you saw behind the fence are my kin."

"But why are you bigger than them?"

"Because it takes centuries for us to grow to my size, we start off small like our cousins, but we eventually grow to the size of humans."

"So, what, you're like a thousand years old?"

"Why do you think I always said I'm old?"

"So huemonary have magical powers?"

"Like any other creature. We aren't that much more special than mystical creatures. And we don't use our 'magic' as much as others. Only when we need to set things in order."

"So, you were watching over our family? Is that why you married our mom?"

"Not so much as you guys but your father. I kept watch to make sure he didn't do anything. And when he died, I saw his soul searching for his body. As for your mother, I really do love her. That's why I haven't returned to my world. I gave up everything for her and I plan to keep it that way."

"Okay, so are we going to keep this a secret?"

"If you would, that'd be great. You should head to bed."

"Alright, and by the way, be more open with everyone. I'm not saying tell ma and James your secret but talk a little more and laugh a little."

"I'll try, goodnight."

"One more thing," she said, pointing behind Randy. "James is awake."

"What?!"

CHAPTER TEN
TRAPPED

I was kidnapped. How this happened and why, was unknown. I guess I was one of the unlucky ones. There were about five or six of us. It was a normal thing here for us to be snatched. Few people would help "guttersnipes" like us escape. They thought we deserved to be locked in cells and sold. Our kind was different from everyone else. My parents before they were taken, told me an old wives' tale of a time before the giants appeared. We lived in peace, we were the ones in charge, free to roam wherever without identification. Then out of the sky they came. It was sparse at first, we didn't think much. We in fact welcomed them to our planet. But they began to populate and develop. They grew bigger, stronger and wiser. They thought they were of a higher species than us and began to trap and sell us for their own pleasures.

I'm beside the point of this story. I don't quite remember everything, but I remember talking with my friends in an alley when the white van appeared. We got a bad feeling and decided it would be best for us to run. Before I could move, I was trapped in a net and dragged inside. It was dark, but I could hear the cries from the others. Many begged to be free, and others cried for their futures and the futures of their children and family left behind. I never knew what the life of a giant was like or what actually happened to those taken. The ones I saw following them obediently were the ones that confused me. Maybe they were brainwashed, or they really liked those people. Whatever the case, I didn't want anything to do with it. When we reached the building, I knew we were going to hell.

The building was lifeless, the outside was gray, the windows were gray, and the inside was gray. On the inside were doctors waiting to exam us. We were made sterile, IDed and shoved into jail cells. Days and weeks passed as we were picked off one by one. I prayed my time would never come. The cries and screams from those around me made it hard to ignore the reality we faced.

The giants cooed and awed at our fear. In all honesty, you can take this however you want, these giants were just repulsive. They sat pretty while they tortured us. Every day another unfortunate soul was forced here. Some talked about life with their giants. These stories whether good or bad to them, disgusted me.

But here, I will give the run down for what happened. A sort of verbal journal to give awareness for what it was like here for us lowly beings.

Day One: I sat in the corner, refusing to eat. The food was suspicious, definitely not something even they would eat. I couldn't trust the food was not poisoned. It seemed after everyone ate, they became too trusting of the people that just violated them. No way would I eat this crap.

Day Two: They still tried to make me taste that crap. When they realized I wouldn't eat they took me to a grey room and examined my body. They felt something was wrong. When the results came back negative, I was sent to my cell. One of these days I planned to escape, how was unknown. I couldn't trust these giant-loving swine to rat me out, so I kept to myself.

Day Five: I met a girl named Juliet. She had beautiful blue eyes and blonde hair. We became friends immediately. We spent the whole day talking. Towards the end, she talked about the giants that tortured and abandoned her.

"They were really good to me," she said. "I was pampered and loved."

"If you were loved, why would they hurt you?"

"I don't know why, they got another one and didn't need me no more."

"So, they didn't love you that much."

"They did, they did! I know they did," she hollered.

"Okay, well what was it like with them."

"Just wonderful, they gave me lots of good food, toys and when I did somethin' right, they gave me more stuff."

"So, you were entertainment?"

"I don't know about that, but I loved bein' with them."

As she said that the giant that fed us came with food. Juliet inhaled it, I looked in complete disgust.

"How can you stomach that crap?"

"It's delicious. Once you eat it, you can't stop. Try it."

"No, I'm good."

"I wish I was over there. I could take that."

Day Seven: Juliet became dearer to me. When you're trapped in a cell for so long, you crave companionship, and she was that person for me. I knew from the start she was a good person. Naïve but kind. She was quite the woman. She was definitely loyal to giants, but she wasn't completely disconnected with her kind. I wished her the best. And maybe one day, we could escape together. We wouldn't be able to have children, but we could adopt the children whose parents disappeared.

I trusted her and decided to tell her my plan of escape. She disagreed and told me it was a horrible idea. That the giants would catch me before I could get passed the first door. But I insisted we escaped and soon.

"Look, it's not safe out there. The giants protect us from it."

"You really are brainwashed huh," I said, appalled at her statement.

How could the giants who kidnapped us in the first place be the ones protecting us? From what? Pizza boxes?

"All I'm sayin' is they won't hurt us. You have to trust'em more."

"I can't trust someone that locks me in a prison cell and feeds me slop."

The conversation ended, and I felt a little betrayed she didn't want to go along.

Day Nine: All day, I had a weird feeling. A sense of dread something bad would happen. Juliet didn't pay much attention to my worries, she said nothing bad would happen. But no matter how much she stated that, I wouldn't shake this feeling. And like that, it happened. I begged they wouldn't do it, but no one listened. It was as a simple joke, they weren't supposed to take it seriously.

We called over giants and began to laugh and be playful. But the giants enjoyed Juliet's performance and took her. As they carried her away, I shouted and begged them to bring her back. To take me as her replacement. But all for nothing.

Day Eleven: I'm malnourished, the bowl of food, looked tempting but I couldn't become one of these brainwashed people. The water looked good, I hadn't had a single drop since well, before I was kidnapped. I licked my lips at the food that once looked disgusting and rotted. It became a luxurious feast. To keep myself from temptation, I thought of Juliet and slept off my hunger.

Day Fourteen: Once again, I'm taken to the room and examined. They couldn't find anything wrong with me. This time, I came to in the room. I could hear their conversation.

"I can't find anything wrong with his results."

"There has to be some reason he's not eating."

"Poor boy, maybe he's just sad. Remember Juliet? Maybe he's upset over her?"

"That could be it, a lot of dogs when they lose a friend will refuse to eat. We just need to give him an IV for now. And hopefully get him a person soon."

"I have an idea, but you should put him back first."

The giant put his hand on my head before taking me back.

Day Fifteen: The giant that cleaned our cells and fed us begged me to eat. Why he was so desperate was beyond me. Maybe he got punished for not completing his tasks. Whatever it was, sucked to be him. I lay back down and slept. Suddenly he opened my cage and I sat up.

"What are you doing? Get out," I shouted.

But he couldn't understand me. He just whispered for me to calm down and reached inside. He grabbed my mouth and I tried to pull away. But like any giant he was strong. He opened my mouth and shoved food inside. The texture went down slimy, but in a second, it was actually good. In an instant, I scarfed down the food.

Day Sixteen: A family of ugly giants were standing in front of me. They found me cute, and adorable. I looked from each giant to the next, and one face looked familiar. It was the man that took Juliet! Rage swelled as he pointed toward me. Soon, the cell cleaner took me out of the cage and put something around my neck.

"Just wait for me to get out of here," I thought.

They put me in a weird shaped van and took me to some building. As I looked out the window, I could see a lot of my kind playing, walking, and using the restroom in public, it was a shocking sight. We then reached their building. What they called a house, and they took me inside.

Inside, someone rushed up to me. It was Juliet. And I became really happy.

"Juliet! You're okay," I said, nuzzling her.

"I told you everythin' would be alright. Now we have the same giants."

"Yeah, that's one bright side to this hellhole. But it'll definitely be easier to escape from here."

"You're joking."

"Not in the slightest, I don't trust them."

Ever since, it's been pretty fun. It wasn't as bad as the others made it appear. We got to leave every so often to use the bathroom, but I peed on the floor, if I wasn't allowed to use their toilet, I wasn't going to pee anywhere else. The food wasn't bad, but their food was way better, and Juliet and I were having fun playing together. I eventually planned to run away, but not for a while.

CHAPTER ELEVEN
THE CURSED BOY

Johann watched Vogel as he softly petted the bird. His eyes slowly closed, as the bird had finally risen. Johann for once in a long time felt sadness for a human as Vogel's heart came to a stop. Johann reached down to unwrap the bandages around the bird's wings. As he opened the window, he remembered his past.

Johann was abandoned at a very young age. He was cursed—or so the villagers thought. Born on the day his birth village held a ritual for the death of a mother who returned to kill children of the village that wrongfully murdered her family. To appease the vengeful spirit, a child had to be sacrificed. It was just coincidence that the child's mother went into labor. When he was born his eyes held the entire forest. Reflected in the child's eyes, the parents could see the forest, the people walking nearby, the blowing leaves, and for that he was unwanted, his parents willingly gave him to the village.

The elders sat the child on a basket, he smiled unknowing of his fate. The new people chanted and danced around him. The bright orange light reflected in his eyes a burning forest. The chief lit the basket on fire. While the child burned, they celebrated and cheered, they casted off the evil spirit. Not a care in the world.

Towards the end of the night, a villager heard the cry of a baby and walked to the fire pit. There he lay, not a scratch on him. The villager screamed and told the chief and the elders about the child that cried in the pit.

"The child is a vengeful spirit," the villager exclaimed.

The elders called a meeting and discussed what to do with the child. By no means could he stay in the village, but on the other hand the gods must have saved him for a reason. It was decided the child would stay until he was a man. In the meantime someone was to take care of him. It was in fact the parents' responsibility had the child not been born on the day of ritual. As ordered, the parents took care of him. The parents did not care for him, so he was never given a name. He was only referred to as You, Child and Boy.

It became known when the child was 4 years old, he was cursed. It was a winter evening, the parents had finally warmed up to the child. During a blizzard—possibly the deadliest storm they ever had. The child wandered from their hut and came across a wolf that was injured. He did not want the doggy to die, so he wished hard enough to save it. But to save a life, one must be lost, equivalent exchange. Because the child saved the wolf, another child died. The parents searched hours after the storm died down for the child. When they found him, he rested peacefully with the wolf. He did not have the proper attire to survive. Fear struck the child's parents, he was truly cursed. He was not human. They looked at the sleeping child and wondered if it would be best to leave him. They looked at each other and nodded, then slowly walked away. Unaware that his parents had abandoned him, the child slept peacefully, the wolf watched the parents as they walked to the village.

When the child woke up, he was alone. The wolf left, and it was dark and scary. His eyes that reflected the trees glanced around to figure out how to get home. He wandered.

The child was scared but something told him to keep walking. He returned to the village a few hours later.

When he arrived, it was on fire. Villagers screamed and ran panicked. Wolves attacked the village. The wolf followed the path the parents took. Pools of blood were on the ground, lifeless bodies laid in front of him. He looked around in fear. In his eyes the trees appeared to have blood sprawled upon the leaves and branches. The child had a dream, one where he feared his parents had died. In his nightmare, he wished they survived. It appeared his nightmare came true. The boy stood still, he did not know what to do. His mother ran across the village in search for his father, there she glanced to see the child had made it to the village.

"*This is all HIS fault,*" she thought.

He was mad they abandoned him and came back for revenge.

The child's mother ran around the village, telling them the child did this. That he wanted revenge and was killing everyone. He needed to die. A vengeful or cursed child should not be in this village, they needed to rest in the ground. The villagers grabbed their weapons and came for him. He stood shocked at what was happening. Why were the villagers angry? They were scaring him. The child ran and ran and hid inside a tree. There he was safe. He clutched his knees and cried. The child rested there for hours, maybe even days. When he felt safe, he crawled out and headed in the direction away from the village. Afraid and hungry he continued to walk.

Along the way he came across an elderly couple. They took the child in. He did not know how to speak, so they did not know his name.

After a lot of consideration, they named him Johann. Because the child had survived so long without food and water, he was blessed. And he was a blessing to the couple that was never able to have a child. They finally had an heir to take over their farm. The couple loved his eyes, he was truly a blessing. His eyes were a confirmation, the beautiful trees whose leaves blew in the wind, brought peace to the couple.

Johann learned to speak, he learned love and warmth. He was happy. His eyes were bright, and in his eyes, sunlight shined through the leaves on the trees.

By the time Johann was 6, his new mother became sick. It was known to his new father that his mother was soon to die. Johann watched as his father sat beside his mother's bed. He prayed and kissed the woman who had become very ill. Johann didn't want his mommy to die so he wished hard. So hard, he begged that she would survive. As the father slept beside the woman who had just passed, Johann walked over and kissed her forehead. Just as he did, her eyes opened. Astonished, she looked from Johann to her husband who slept deeply.

Confused as to why she had so much energy, she spoke quietly to herself, "Why am I still alive?"

Johann heard and responded, "Because I wished mommy was okay."

It became clear to his mother he was special. She remembered a story she heard, of a cursed child from a village not too far, in his eyes were trees. He killed a child, and then set wolves on the village after being abandoned. She spoke to Johann and told him never to wish for things again. And never speak of this to anyone, not even daddy. Johann promised.

When Johann's mother went outside to milk their cow, she looked over to see a lot of their chickens had died. It was very strange, but she thought nothing of it. Her chickens were very unhealthy due to their farm's low income. It was natural for a random number to die in a week. But so many at once, was something new.

Johann and his new family continued to live a happy life until he reached 15. Along the way, Johann's mother figured he was ready to interact with the village. He became an adored member, and a great asset. He was the youngest man in the village and most capable of hunting and field work. Johann's parents were given numerous offerings of arranged marriages. They believed life couldn't be any better. But they knew Johann had his eyes on one girl, Annelise. Annelise was the daughter of the village doctor. The most respected family in their village, even above the chief's.

She was beautiful, talented, and fluent in many languages. Every young male in the village was in love with her. She was the ideal wife. She was "exotic", her brown skin, dark wavy hair, slim physique, and sweet personality were bonuses. Johann and Annelise spent a great deal of time together, Johann's parents waited for when the doctor would ask for their engagement. It was assured.

Although Johann was loved, he was also despised. One man in particular, detested even the sight of him. His name was Sebastian, son of the chief. He was jealous of Johann. Sebastian was supposed to be the asset of the village. Not an adopted farm boy. But what really infuriated Sebastian, was the relationship Johann held with Annelise. The chance of them wedding was higher, and everyone knew it. Sebastian felt entitled. He was given everything from a young age and got away with anything. He expected their marriage, demanded it daily with his father.

However, each day Johann and Annelise would sneak off to an old mill miles away. There, they would talk until sunset. They were in love. They wanted no more than to be together forever. One day, Annelise couldn't take it anymore.

"Johann, we should run away. My parents don't realize I want to marry you."

"We can't," Johann responded. "My parents are old. They need me to take over their farm. I am their only child."

"The farm isn't doing well, it's sure to die over soon. We can leave a note for them. They would understand."

"I can't. They took me in, took care of me. I owe them everything."

"Please Johann. I feel they want me to marry the chief's son."

"Let's think about it. We'll go home tonight, and if nothing changes in a week, I will consider."

Two days went by, and Johann heard a knock on his door. It was Annelise.

"We have to talk," Annelise said, walking into his home.

"Can this wait," Johann whispered. "My parents are asleep, and it's not appropriate for you to visit me at this hour. If we're caught—"

"Shh, if you don't want anything to happen then let me in your room."

Johann sighed and led her to his room.

"What did you want to talk about."

"Let's run away," Johann rolled his eye and stood up. And Annelise said quickly, "Please hear me out, yes, we agreed to wait a week, but my parents accepted the offer from the chief. I don't want to marry Sebastian."

"Calm down, can't you explain to your father you're in love with me?"

"Not everyone's parents are as understanding as yours," she disparaged.

"I know, but sometimes it doesn't hurt to try."

"Look, my father isn't like that. He's loyal to the chief. He won't change his mind. Please, I love you. We leave tonight and not a soul can stop us."

"And what about the reprimands my parents would face. Not only had their son eloped, but he did it with the chief's daughter-in-law. I can't have them suffer for my selfishness."

"They'll be fine, we can leave a note explaining, and demand they don't punish them."

Johann was not convinced he should leave his parents. Annelise felt betrayed.

"Are you really choosing your family over me?"

"I'm sorry, they saved my life. I owe them my entire world," he said.

"You'll regret this," Annelise said, as she cried. "You'll regret ever breaking my heart."

She stormed out of the house, Johann felt bad for hurting her, but he loved his parents more. He decided to apologize in the morning.

That night, Johann dreamt a disaster fell upon the village. As he stood there, tied to a post he watched Annelise burn near the village square. Trapped. Johann was startled awake, an ill feeling made his stomach churn and he walked to the window. In the distance was a red glow, instinctively he ran to the village.

When he arrived, the village was on fire. The villagers screamed and abandoned their homes. Parents searched for their children. Johann ran to the closest villager and asked what happened.

"We don't know," he said. "The doctor's house burst into flames, and the fire spread quickly."

"Are they alright?"

"Everyone but Annelise. They haven't been able to find—hey!"

Johann sprinted full speed to their home.

"Annelise," he yelled running into the flames. "Think, what happened in the dream. Where was she? The square!"

Johann ran to the square. Nothing was there. Suddenly he was ambushed from behind.

"If I can't have her, no one can," the voice said.

Johann was pushed to a pole and tied up. There he saw Sebastian and a few other men smirking at his demise. Sebastian rounded up those that despised him to kill him. He fought as best he could. He saw movement to his right, Annelise was being dragged to the square.

"Now," Sebastian yelled. "You have one choice! You can agree to marry me, and I let him go, or you can perish with him."

"Do as he says," Johann said.

"I can't," she cried. "I'd rather die here than marry him."

"Please," Johann begged. "It's not worth it."

Annelise stayed silent.

"Should've listened to lover boy," Sebastian said, shoving her in a heap of wood and buried her. "Could have had it all."

A pair of hands covered Johann's eyes, "We won't force you to see this before you die too."

Sebastian set the pile on fire. Johann struggled to break free as Annelise screamed in pain. Tears streamed down his face.

4 hours later, the only thing left was Johann. The village was destroyed, and no one remained. He stood over the fire pit, emotionless. He lost his will.

"*Why does everything go wrong?*" He thought.

"Because you allow it," a voice said, from behind. "Things go wrong for you because you don't use that gift you have."

"Who are you?" he asked startled.

It was a man, he paced around the square, "A no one, like you."

Johann looked into his eyes, that reflected a raging storm, "Well surely you have a name."

"Maybe I do, maybe I don't, call me whatever you want."

"I'll call you A," he said.

"What a strange name," A said, astounded.

"Well, if you want a better one, tell me yours."

"No need," A retorted. "I won't be here long."

"Then why are you here?"

"Just to let you know, you can change the outcome of this," A said, walking to the fire pit. "You can bring her back at the expense of another life."

"If what you say is true, why do I need to kill someone to bring her back."

"It's simple. You cannot bring a spirit back to life without taking another. It's called Equivalent Exchange. Why it works that way you'll have to discover on your own. The universe works in mysterious ways, one change, no matter how significant or insignificant it is, will throw the universe off track. And that can't happen. So, if it's worth it, save her."

"Can I choose who to sacrifice?"

"Oooh, a little revenge I see?" A said excitedly, his eyes which held a raging storm now filled with flames. "You can, just think of him, and grant her his life. Oh, and by the way, considering she'll be coming back from nothing, there's a 10% chance of her ever remembering you. Good luck."

"Wait you're leaving?" Johann asked.

"Yeah, I did my job. Spread my knowledge to another one of us, I'm off the clock."

"But what am I?"

"You'll have to figure that out yourself."

With that, A left. Johann stood conflicted. He wanted his revenge against Sebastian. But if he brought back Annelise, she wouldn't remember him. Could he bear to live with that? Johann closed his eye. He thought about Sebastian as her sacrifice.

"Bring her back to life," he thought.

A light appeared over the rubble and faded away.

"Annelise?" Johann called gently.

Movement pushed the wood pile. And out appeared a woman.

"Who...are you?" he asked.

"Mia, the gardener's daughter. Who are you?"

"It doesn't matter, are you alright?" he asked extending his hand.

"I'm okay," she said, taking his hand.

"How did you end up down here?"

"I really shouldn't say," she said.

"Please, I'd like to know. I'm searching for someone."

"The chief's son, Sebastian and I were in love. He promised me marriage, but his father refused my parent's offer. And we were upset. We promised to set the village on fire and die together. I was first but, I survived. Is Sebastian safe?" she asked grabbing Johann's clothes.

"I'm not sure, can you please continue on?"

"That's all I remember. Though I think one girl asked to join in to fake her own death. And we agreed."

"So, she faked it," Johann sighed. "I must get going. I have to find out if my parents are alive. Good luck finding Sebastian or whatever else."

Johann ran for his parents' farm. When he arrived, all their livestock were slaughtered, and lain injured were his parents.

"Mother, father," he rushed to them. "Are you okay?"

Johann begged his parents were okay. He didn't want to use his power, but if he had to, he knew who to exchange. He shook his father, no response. He lifted him up and under was a pool of blood.

"No," Johann whispered. "Please, no."

He ran to his mother, she was still breathing but was weak, "Hold on."

Johann carefully carried his mother inside and laid her on the bed, then his father. He placed his hand on his father's head, weakly his mother watched. Johann took a deep breath and thought about Annelise's betrayal. He decided to use the people who attacked him to bring his father back and extend his parents' lives.

Johann's father opened his eyes and jumped up. He looked around the room, and asked Johann, "What happened? I was sure I'd died."

Johann remembered what his mother said but it was time his father knew what he could do.

"Mother told me never to tell you," Johann said. "And I'm sorry mother for telling him, but at this point, he should know."

"Know what?" his father asked.

"I have a sort of 'power', I can bring people back to life in exchange for another life. I don't know much about it, and I need to find out what I can do. But that's why mother survived that illness 10 years ago. I was told never to speak about it, because before I met you and mother, I was hated by my birth parents. And they spread rumors of me being a vengeful spirit, so mother said to keep it secret."

His father was silent before saying, "So you have powers...That's cool. I wish I'd grown up with that kind of power."

"It's not weird?" Johann asked.

"Not in the least. You're our son, we will never hate you."

Johann was relieved. And now it was time to test his theory of extending their life. He wasn't entirely sure of how to do this, but he was willing to do anything to keep them alive.

"Father, please hold mother's hand."

"What's going on?" he asked grabbing his wife's hand

"I'm not sure how to do this, but I want to extend yours and mother's lives by 50 years."

Johann's parents laughed.

"That is a sweet gesture," his mother said, weakly.

"But we have lived 70 years, we still have 30 years to go. The point of life is to eventually die. We're not afraid of it."

"But," Johann said. "I don't want you to."

Johann's father placed his arm on Johann's shoulder, "I know, but that's also life. To lose those special. I lost my parents, your mother did, it eventually happens to everyone."

Johann looked down and avoided eye contact, "There was more to this, I have to leave. I need to find out what I am. So, I wanted to keep you alive, so I could come back. I hate leaving you."

"It's okay, go and find out. Visit us time to time."

Johann nodded and kissed his mother, then hugged his father.

"I should get going," he said.

Johann left his home and the burned village. He learned about the world, and in turn was hated wherever he went. Through simple mistakes he saved and ended lives. But he learned how to use his strengths and fate had a way to change his life forever.

At the end of his first journey, he crossed the village where he was born. There, he saw his birth mother and father. And they recognized him too. Cautiously, Johann walked past them. His eyes didn't leave them until he was a safe distance away. When he faced forward, he was hit with a hard object.

"The cursed boy is back," a villager yelled.

"You killed my son," another stated.

"It's time we got revenge for what you did!"

Johann was beaten and thrown out of the village. He limped to his parents' farm and knocked on the door.

A stranger answered, "Can I help you?"

"Who are you?" he asked. "Where is the elderly couple that live here?"

"They passed not too long ago. Their son was gone so the chief gave the place to us. Are you their son?"

Johann ignored the stranger and walked away. He was too shocked to think. He had nowhere to go. If only he visited his parents earlier. Johann sat under a tree and looked at the sky. Why was he cursed? His eyes that could see the forests, only caused him pain and sadness.

His pain and sadness led to anger. And he saw a bird, it was beautiful, different from the others, but the passing strangers admired it.

"Why is it okay for the bird who's just as different as me, adored by everyone," Johann thought. "Why do I suffer while it lives a carefree life? If it wants to be that way, it can just die!"

Johann ended the bird's life, he didn't believe something like that should be treated better than him, a human. Johann looked at the bird, and instantly, guilt flooded his emotions. What had he done? He took an innocent life out of envy. He wished he could change what was done, but if what he was learning was true, there was no way to bring it back to life without a sacrifice.

Injured, he walked to a close village and asked to see a doctor. He didn't have money and was turned away. The doctor told him to see a doctor named Vogel but warned him he was a dangerous person.

Confused, Johann set for Dr. Vogel. Was Vogel like him? A cursed being? Maybe he could explain more to him. He didn't know where to find him. And his wounds were getting worse. He wandered the village hoping to find him.

He asked strangers that looked at him in disgust, to no avail. Finally, a kind old woman told him he lived in the forest as a hermit. Johann thanked the woman and walked into the forest.

He walked forever through the paths, until one day, he saw an old man that found the dead bird.

"I better take him back," the man said.

"Why is he taking it home?" Johann thought. He knew it was dead. But he wondered why the man would try to help a bird.

For now, Johann walked away. His guilt for hurting the bird made it harder to face the man who was trying to save it. He decided it would be best for his injuries to heal on their own. He needed a place to hide and rest, when he remembered the mill wasn't too far from there.

I can stay there until I heal, he thought.

When Johann arrived at the old mill, there stood A waiting for him. Johann slowed to a stop before him.

"You don't look so good," A said, sarcastically.

"What's to be expected when you're hated by the whole world?"

"Ohh, not the whole world, but a good chunk of it."

"Why are you here?"

"Because I wanted to see how you were doing," he said.

"How did you know I was here?"

"Ah, ha ha. You still haven't figured everything out in 10 years," A laughed. "You're the slowest out of all of us. Have you figured out what you are?"

Johann shook his head faintly.

A scoffed, "Here I am doing you a favor and you can't even figure out anything."

"I haven't met anyone but you. So, there's no way I can figure out what we are."

"You haven't gotten anything?" A asked. "No dreams, signs, nothin'?"

Johan shook his head.

"No wonder you murdered that poor bird," A snarled. "If you'd known, you wouldn't kill."

"How did you know I—?"

A shook his head disappointedly, "You're a lost cause. I can't explain anything to you until you figure out what you are."

A stormed away leaving Johann stunned.

What had he done to incite so much anger in him? Was that bird really that important? Johann thought about what A said. He tried to think back on what his signs could have been.

Johann sat by the stream, reminiscing about his life. Where did this all go wrong? If only he and Annelise had never met. The village wouldn't have burned, he would still live a sheltered safe life in the village that accepted who he was. Johann sighed and played with his reflection in the stream.

He was going to find Dr. Vogel. His injuries were better, but he still needed answers and Dr. Vogel seemed to be the one.

Johann made his way to the path to Dr. Vogel. He didn't know which way to turn when he saw Vogel with a smile on his face and in a hurry. He wanted to call out to him, but he couldn't trust it. He was just a human, nothing like him.

"Good afternoon," Dr. Vogel said. "It's a lovely day."

Astonished, Johann mumbled, "Yes."

He couldn't find it in him to ask for help. But he wanted to find where he lived so he followed him. He watched from the window, the look of disappointment on Dr. Vogel's face seeing the bird still sleep. Johann decided to come back tomorrow.

A day went by, and all Johann could think about was Vogel and the bird. He went back to Vogel's cottage. He saw him praying by the window and he heard his prayer to save the bird. Johann walked away.

"Hey," someone called out from behind. "You the one that's friends with the cursed freak?"

"What cursed freak?" Johann asked turning around.

The 4 strangers winced at Johann.

"Ugh," one said. "What the hell is wrong with his eyes?"

"Lets just get this over with," another said.

Johann looked to their hands to see they had weapons. He wasn't surprised, but the last thing he needed was another beating, he ran away.

"Hey," they yelled.

Johann ran as fast as he could, but his injuries were slowing him down. He tried to think of ways he could use his gifts without resorting to killing them. Not paying attention to his surroundings, Johann tripped over the now vine filled ground.

"You made us have to run," one said. "You just made it harder for yourself."

Johann was beaten horribly. When the strangers finished, Johann was left with serious bleeding, and he could barely move. He needed to get back to Vogel. No way was he going to make it to the old mill like this. Johann forced himself up, and slowly walked to Vogel's cottage.

It was the next day when Johann reached Vogel's door. He knocked and waited for him to answer. Johann was nervous. He couldn't bear to see the bird. It was his fault all of this happened.

I should turn back, Johann thought.

But it was too late. Vogel opened the door. And with speed helped Johann inside.

"Please sit down," Vogel said.

Johann sat down, "I don't have any money to pay."

"Don't worry," Vogel said, grabbing his medical kit.

As Vogel stitched Johann's wounds, Johann stared at the bird. *Was he treated like this?*

When Vogel finished, he smiled.

"Your injuries weren't that severe," Vogel said. "Your arm is broken, and you have very minor stomach bleeding. Take these for the next 3 weeks and you will be fine."

"Thank you, Doctor," Johann said, taking the medicine bag. "Usually people fear me. Turn a blind eye to whenever someone attacks. Turning me away at their doors, running in fear. Really, thank you. If there is anything I can do for you as a way of gratitude—"

"No," Vogel said, as humble as ever. "There is no need to repay me."

"Okay," Johann said. "If ever you decide to seek something, I live in the old mill, by valley falls. My name is Johann."

Johann felt attached to the kind old man, it may have been one-sided, but he liked Dr. Vogel.

As he left the cottage, Vogel returned to caring for the bird. Johann glanced back at Dr. Vogel.

"Even after caring for me, he went back to the bird," Johann thought. It had been so

long since he saw someone ever be kind towards him or any other in years.

"Is he okay?" Johann asked returning to Vogel.

"No," Vogel said. "He hasn't woken up in over a month. I've tried every possible way for him to wake but nothing's happened. I fear he's soon to die."

"Has it really been a month," Johann mumbled.

He watched Vogel as his eyes lowered in pain. Why was the bird so important? Johann sighed.

"There is a way," Johann hesitated.

"What do you mean?" Vogel said, a bit of hope in his eyes. "Please tell me. I'll do anything."

Johann stood in silence before continuing, "It would be at the cost of your life."

Johann saw the despair on Vogel's face.

Dr. Vogel asked why he had to give his life, and though Johann only knew the basics, he explained in a way that appeared as if he knew everything.

Guilty for giving him such a harsh decision, Johann said goodbye and headed to the old mill.

Johann waited for Vogel to appear, it was taking a while for him to come. And Johann's expectations were low. Why would he give his life to save a bird? There were so many people that needed to be treated, why would he die for one bird?

Johann heard the faint sound of his name being called.

"Johann! I've made up my mind. I ask for this one favor! Johann!"

Johann was shocked, he was really giving up his life. He left the mill.

"Are you sure?" he asked, genuinely worried. "You'll die in return."

"Yes," he replied. "If it will save his life, I will give mine."

"As you wish. When you enter, go to the bird and there I will give your life to him."

Johann followed Vogel to the cottage. There the bird rested on the windowsill.

"Are you ready," Johann asked.

"Yes," Dr. Vogel said, walking over to the bird.

Dr. Vogel got onto his knees and gently petted the bird. Johann observed, he never thought there would be a human that would ever give for another, especially for a bird.

"What a truly sad thing," he thought. *"Do only the kind die?"*

Johann walked over to Vogel and closed his eyes. As Johann ended Vogel's life, his chest ached.

Johann watched the bird as it flew away. Its life was extended for 10 years. Johann didn't know what to do with Vogel. He took the old man to his bed and placed the blanket over him.

"I'm sorry," Johann said. "This was all my fault. If I never killed it in the first place, you wouldn't have died. I am so sorry."

"So, you finally see your fault?" a voice asked.

Johann turned around, it was A, "How do you know where I am?"

"Still don't know?" he asked.

"I don't, I was raised by normal people. I don't know what signs to look for, or how to figure out who I am."

A sighed, "Alright, I'll tell you."

A motioned for Johann to sit at the table.

He continued, "We are foreseers for the universe. You hold more power than you think you've learned. You can do so much with just so little. You can watch over humans, decide if you want their life to end, and a lot more."

"So, I'm an Angel?" Johann asked.

"Angel? No, they do similar work, but we are able to be seen by humans, interact with them, and alternate things of our own accord. Though sometimes we can get in trouble too."

"So, this whole time, I could have saved the bird and not have taken his life?"

"Correct, I figured you would learn the correct way, but instead you gave him the death option."

"If I have so much power, is there a way I can bring him back?"

"There is," A said. "You can give your life for his."

Johann flinched, "So the same thing he did?"

A nodded.

Johann thought hard, this was all his fault. He could make up for it by giving him his life. He could be with his parents again. Safe and loved.

Johann nodded, "I'll do it."

A erupted in laughter, "Your face is so serious. Do you really think you'll die?"

Johann's face tensed.

"Relax, you're immortal. If you 'give your life' you come back to life right away. It's a simple trick foreseers use to bring others to life. Are you up to trying it?"

"Yes," Johann said.

"Just give your life to him."

"Can I ask, why are you helping me?"

"It was my error that you ended up with the wrong family. So, I tried to help as much as I could."

"Why did you take so long to help me and then tell me to figure it out myself?"

"I underestimated, your abilities. Anyways get along with it, can't take too long to revive him. When you're back, come with me and I'll teach you everything."

"And what about Vogel? Doesn't he become immortal because he took my life?"

"He will, but that will be his choice to do with it as he pleases."

Johann walked to Dr. Vogel and placed his hand on him and took a deep breath. Johann collapsed, and Dr. Vogel opened his eyes.

Confused, he said, "But...I thought I died?"

"You did," A said. "But the kid brought you back."

Dr. Vogel looked at Johann and checked his pulse, "He's...dead."

"He'll be fine," A said. "He's immortal."

"I-mmortal?" Vogel asked. "So, he will wake up?"

"Eventually."

"Do you mind helping me place him on the bed?"

"You have that much energy after *JUST* being resurrected?" A asked astonished. "I can help, but usually people can't move for days."

"I guess I'm an exception," Dr. Vogel laughed. "I am Friedrich Vogel, and you are?"

"Oh, just a kind friend of Johann's. Don't bother with me."

Vogel nodded and grabbed Johann. They put him on the bed.

Dr. Vogel prepared food, "Is there anything you would like to have?"

"Oh, I'm fine," A said. "Johann should be waking up soon. So, he could probably use some food."

Dr. Vogel and A talked while Johann slept.

2 hours later, Johann woke up.

"You're awake," Dr. Vogel said. "I made dinner."

"Thank you," Johann said. "But I'm not hungry."

"I understand," Vogel said, disappointedly.

"Come now," A said. "You should eat something before we go."

"I'm fine," Johann mumbled.

"He went through a lot to make this," A said. "Especially for you."

"I'm not hungry."

"It's fine," Vogel interrupted. "It doesn't matter."

"Fine then," A said. "Let's go."

"What about him?" Johann asked.

A looked at Vogel, "It's up to you. You're also immortal, so you have a lot of time on your hand."

"Why doesn't he come with us?" Johann asked. "He also needs to learn everything too."

Dr. Vogel stood silently. He was too in shock to comprehend what was going on.

"Such a selfless act, you were rewarded. To give your life for a little creature who wouldn't live for 10 years. You are truly something," A said. "You aren't at the level we are, but you have the power to fix life. You can come with us and learn what your power is or stay here and live the life you had before."

"Come with us," Johann said. "Learn how to use those powers."

"I...don't know..." Vogel said. "This seems like a lot."

"It is," A said. "But just get used to it."

Dr. Vogel waited before nodding his head, "I'll go."

Johann smiled, all of the trouble he caused was finally turning out alright. Johann, A and Dr. Vogel walked out of the house to begin their training.

Johann was able to control his powers and gain new ones. And Dr. Vogel, he became a lower-level foreseer, that cured the ill. He became a legend, a god to the villages. He was worshipped and praised. He was finally noticed for who he truly was.

The ones that were cursed, lived the happiest lives.

CHAPTER TWELVE
DANCE WITH THE FAIRIES OF DEATH.

While you sleep, under your bed waits a fairy for your time of death. The story I'm about to tell, is just a little warning for those who ever dare mess with a fairy of death's work.

Timothy Wallace was a man who feared death. Every night he took precautions to make sure his heart would not stop. He made sure every door and every window in the house was locked. Placed in his bed side drawer were a gun and knife. He lived his life fearing the unknown, if a stranger walked 10 feet from him, he ran or jumped to defense. But no matter how cautious a person can be, death still lingered. Waiting for the opportune moment to strike.

Wallace lay in bed. His fatigue was too overwhelming. After a long day of reports and his boss bellowing at him, he was too tired to do his daily checks and fell asleep.

And with carelessness comes danger. The fairy in wait had its opportunity to finish its job. It waited too long to finish Wallace and now was finally its chance.

The fairy thought of a reasonable way to kill Wallace. What did he have for dinner? Just its luck, Wallace was too tired to cook so he brought home your average greasy fast food.

As Wallace slept, peaceful as he had ever been, the fairy crept onto his bed. Its black wings and wand blending into the fairly dark room. It prepared its wand to stick into his heart. The fairy checked to see if Wallace was in a deep enough sleep to climb onto his chest rather than fly over. Seemed like it. The fairy climbed onto Wallace's chest, its tiny footsteps barely noticeable. It crept as quietly as possible.

As the fairy reached its destination, it glanced to see that Wallace was awake. Staring at the unknown creature on his left breast. The fairy still as could be waited for Wallace to fall back asleep. Little to be known, Wallace had a different plan.

Wallace reached under his pillow slowly to make sure the fairy did not leave. And out he pulled a small glass cage. Wallace carefully moved his arm, making sure the fairy did not see. And with a swift movement, threw the cage on top of the fairy. The fairy kicked and punched, trying its very best to escape. Wallace made sure the cage was sealed tightly before lighting the fireplace. He looked down at the creature. It looked like the shadow of a toy casting from the light of the fire. The fairy looked up at Wallace, it seemed to be communicating, possibly begging for its life. Wallace didn't care. All he knew was that if he set it free, it would kill him eventually.

"I'm sorry," he said, throwing the fairy into the fire.

Wallace watched as the fairy's body burned, the look of sheer agony on its face. Before long, the glass shattered, and flames engulfed the fairy.

Wallace was proud, relieved, that he killed the thing responsible for his death. He gave a slight smile and went back to bed, after of course doing his nightly checks.

Earlier, while at work, Wallace came across an article. A man spoke of the "invisible fairies" that were responsible for each person's death. The man later died of unknown causes. And to Wallace, that was proof enough to fear these new causes of death. Wallace researched and devised a plan on how to capture and kill his fairy. The article spoke of a specific cage that was required to catch a fairy. From the very little research Wallace did, he did not gather any details on what happened after a fairy was dead. Wallace went on with his life as if nothing happened.

The fairy may die, but it is never the end to its killer's fate. When a fairy dies, a message is sent from the one who watches each fairy. He warns the others about the killer and to watch out. This however was a strange occurrence, the last a fairy was killed was over 5,000 years ago. When humans knew about mystical creatures, and believed they were around. The messenger of death was very wary about the man who killed his most talented fairy. And knew he was dangerous. The fairy sent word to the others, kill Timothy Wallace.

The next day, Wallace woke up to a fresh feeling. He felt there was no danger, that he could restart his life scare free. Do the things he was never able to do.

Wallace walked to work, nothing scared him. He even walked on the side of construction. As he walked under the construction site the rope of an I-beam snapped and fell within 5 feet behind Wallace. Wallace looked back startled, but Wallace feared nothing. He couldn't die, and that to him was a sign of luck. It didn't fall on him, it missed by inches. Death couldn't do its job anymore. Wallace continued on his way to work.

The new confident Wallace walked into the street without looking both ways when a truck came barreling out of nowhere. Lucky for Wallace, his reflexes were quick. Wallace quickly jumped to the side, startled he watched the truck speed off.

"*Asshole,*" Wallace thought.

Again, he paid no attention to the danger that happened. And made his way inside his office building. Wallace never took the elevator. He read those signs "*in case of fire use the stairs,*" and refused to get on one. He also watched movies where people would get stuck and plummet to their deaths. No way would he take those chances. But today of course was different. Death could do nothing to Wallace. It failed numerous times, so why not take the elevator to the 8th floor for once?

Before it rose to the third floor, the elevator was already packed. Wallace looked at the sign that read *weight capacity 2000lbs or 15 persons.* He counted the heads in front of him, there were way more than what the limit warned. Wallace's heart pounded harder and harder.

"*We're going to fall. Please get to the 8th floor soon,*" he thought.

But he remembered he was immortal and relaxed.

"*These people will die of carelessness. Why do I need to worry about them?*"

Just as he thought it, the elevator came to a short halt. And the lights flickered. Even though Wallace was immortal, he still experienced fear. He glanced at the man who kept pressing the call button, though it was obvious all power was off. Suddenly the elevator rumbled and shook. And again, until the last rope holding it up snapped and they fell. The elevator erupted in screams as everyone stumbled around.

Wallace prayed, please let them survive.

It felt as if they were on a drop tower. Wallace felt dizzy and nauseous. The last rope that snapped swung around. It then latched itself to one of the floors. And everyone fell over. No one dared to make a move, until finally a firefighter appeared over to rescue them. Wallace was happy none of them died. Not to mention the gruesome scene he'd have to see and be stuck with until someone came to collect bodies.

The workers were given the option to go home, and all but one stayed. Wallace needed the money. If he were to live forever, he needed money to survive.

Halfway through work his office lit on fire and the entrance was blocked. He couldn't escape, and the flames grew bigger. But to his luck there was a window washer outside. He escaped. After the days problems Wallace was forced to leave.

He was given a ride home. Inside his coworker's car they felt faint, tired, and dizzy, all the symptoms of carbon monoxide. Because Wallace was so cautious, he knew the symptoms by heart and told his coworker to pull over. Wallace decided it was best to walk home. While walking he pondered why he was having so many near death experiences.

Deep in thought, Wallace did not notice the event ahead. A man, tired of struggling in life decided to rob a bank. He was making his way out when Wallace crossed his path. And with a quick motion grabbed him. Wallace felt the muzzle of a gun on his temple as the rather large man wrapped his arm around Wallace's neck.

"Nobody move," the man yelled. "If anyone takes one step closer, I'll blow his brains out!"

"Now now," the new bold Wallace said. "Please don't do anything rash. You see, I cannot die, I'm immortal. So, your threat will become useless once the trigger is pulled."

"Shut it," the man said. "We could test your little theory once I get out of here."

"Once you shoot and I don't go down, it'll be over. Don't be so reckless."

"Let's go," the man said, pulling Wallace back with force.

They rushed behind the side of the building. And into an alley. The man checked to see if anyone followed. The coast was clear.

The man let Wallace go, "Now do you really want to test your theory of being immortal?"

The man aimed towards Wallace.

"Go ahead," Wallace said. His stance was brave, and he stuck his chest out.

"Well, if you say so. I always wanted to shoot a man."

The sound of a gunshot swelled through the alley and the man went down in pain. Shocked Wallace looked and saw a cop standing just behind them.

"You alright?" the officer asked.

"Yes, quite," Wallace replied. "Thank you for helping. Now if you do not mind, I'd like to head home."

"*What a strange day*," he thought.

How many near death experiences could one man have? Would his life as an immortal be this tiresome?

Once Wallace turned onto the path leading to his tiny home, his house burst into flames. Wallace's fear surfaced again. He *MUST* have been assigned a new fairy of death, one less scheming than the other.

His house was gone, where was he going to sleep? Where could he find shelter when death made another appearance? A block from the remnants of his home was a hotel. A safe enough distance to make it inside without dying. Wallace planned to sleep one night there and visit a real estate office the following day.

Wallace was too nervous to sleep. He sat on his bed and watched the door then the window. What could he do? There must have been some way to ease the pressure, lessen the chances of dying. Wallace chose to go to the library and find out.

Later in the morning, Wallace set out to the library. Wallace couldn't find a thing on what happened after a fairy died. In the articles from his previous research, that part was left out. The best Wallace could find was an article that stated moving to a wooded area. Secluded from any possible items that could be dangerous. Wallace sighed and decided to go to the real estate office.

Meanwhile, the messenger of death was furious, how could someone, a human at that, survive a full force of fairies? He needed to cut down on the number of fairies and only assign the smartest. And so, he did. They would not reach Wallace for two weeks, which was a stroke of luck.

Wallace was moved into his new home within 7 hours. So far Wallace experienced no danger. He believed his worries were over. He was completely secluded. No one lived within 10 miles, yet the property kept any animals clear of the vicinity. Wallace packed 6 years' worth of food to minimize the need to return to the city or leave the home.

Wallace enjoyed the comfort of no people to intimidate him, no I-beams or chances of fires to kill him. He was content amidst solitude. Peaceful sleep, time to read, he enjoyed his immortality.

Two weeks went by and still no sign of danger. Wallace was ecstatic. He made his way around death. He would sincerely live forever. Or so he thought.

In the window were three fairies. each figuring out Wallace's patterns and personality and devising a plan. There wasn't much in his home to use to kill him. The only way was scaring him out of the house and be mauled by some animal.

As usual, Wallace finished his book at 8:30 PM and began his health check-ups. As he reached over to grab the band a small fire sparked. Wallace jumped. His heart raced faster and faster. He was confused, how could they find him, why didn't this work? Suddenly many books and lamps began to fall over, causing the fire to spread instantly.

Wallace ran out of the house. Not stopping to look behind him. In the distance, Wallace heard a wolf howling. His heart raced even faster. From every direction he could hear something dangerous. How could animals have gotten through? Wallace ran and ran. These fairies were driving him insane. He just wanted all of this to end. To not be scared anymore.

Wallace kept running until he came across a bridge. On the other side stood three wolves. Their bright blue eyes glared in the moonlight. They walked slowly to him. Before Wallace could run the other direction, he heard the sound of another twig breaking from behind. His options were low. There was no way out. He was for sure dead. Wallace did not want the fairies to have the pleasure of killing him, so he walked to the edge of the bridge. Wallace looked over to see the 30-foot drop. He took one last breath, as he did a small figure came out of the woods from behind. There it stood watching Wallace get ready to jump. It flew over to Wallace and pressed its tiny hand on Wallace's leg and he jumped.

Who was that fairy? None other than the fairy he "killed."

You see, the fairy had gotten bored waiting for a moment to kill him, it knew Wallace had a fear of death. Since a fairy was always around their human, it saw everything. Wallace finding out the truth was a perfect chance for him to die. Why not make a game out of it? The fairy kept Wallace alive just enough to the brink of insanity.

CHAPTER THIRTEEN
THE GRAVEYARD

It was 1983. We just finished our usual rounds around the graveyard. But something in the air was different. Maybe it was the dropping temperatures, or the fact that Dan wasn't complaining about his usual ghost nonsense.... I should go back a bit and introduce Dan and myself.

My name is Greg, at the time, I was 25. It was my first year at the cemetery on 18th St. I got the job through a connection from my uncle, who was great friends with the priest at the church. My partner Dan was in his late twenties. He worked at the cemetery since he was 18. He told me once, that he got this job because he wanted to see if the old myth of Samantha were true. He dedicated his life to finding her. He was lazy and always disappeared when the priest came to tell us what to do. Every night when we made our rounds to check if any kids were in the graveyard, he would tell me a story of some sap that experienced Samantha. But I guess you're wondering who Samantha is?

Samantha E. Garwood was a beautiful woman from the 1800s. She was married to a man named Franklin D. Brown through an arranged marriage. Brown was an awful man who was emotionally and physically abusive towards her. One day, she grew tired of his abuse and decided to run away. She packed her bags and hid them in her personal study and waited for night to escape. While Brown slept, Samantha crept out of bed and headed towards her study. As she grabbed her bags, she heard him stir from his sleep.

"Samantha?" He asked the sound of their bed creaked.

She panicked as he set off searching for her. She threw her bags out of the window and ran towards this cemetery. Brown entered her study to find the window open. He looked out and saw her running.

"Samantha," he yelled, climbing out the window. "Get your ass back here!"

Samantha kept running. She ran into the cemetery and hid behind the biggest tombstone. Brown grabbed a shovel from an undone grave and searched. There he found her, hiding in a fetal position, and beat her to death. They say she still walked the cemetery fearing her husband.

It was a myth. They claimed she appeared every night. I hadn't seen her once. However, Dan believed it and wanted to find her.

But back to the story, the night was strange. Dan was quiet, and something just felt wrong. I couldn't figure out what I was feeling. Every night was okay, normal. But that night was the night everything changed. By the biggest tombstone, I saw a blue light. Its light was a hue like the sky on a sunny day.

"Samantha," Dan whispered. "I found you."

"Dan," I called, as he walked towards the light.

"Samantha, I finally found you."

There behind the tomb was a woman so beautiful I was left speechless. Her skin was a bright blue, her long curly hair dark blue. Her face, something about her expression as she floated there, was mesmerizing. I couldn't explain what it was. Her large eyes were lowered, her lips were full, her nose was small, and her facial structure was slim. She wore a bright blue rag that looked like it could have been white with blue reflections.

"Samantha," Dan said, slowly approaching her. "It's really you. I finally found you."

Samantha's eyes widened with Dan's words.

"Don't come near," she said, backing away.

"Samantha," he replied. "I've been searching for you for over a century. Come here."

Samantha struggled as Dan got closer.

"I didn't mean to hurt you, I love you. You're my beloved wife."

He continued, "Look it's me. Franklin, Frankie. Come here love."

I was confused, what was happening? Dan was spouting garbage about Samantha being his wife and not meaning to hurt her. I was completely frozen, what was going on.

"Dan," I managed to spit out. "What in the hell is going on?"

"Oh, I forgot you were here," Dan said, turning towards me. "This is my wife, Samantha. Due to old events we were separated for a while."

"Dude don't joke around. How can you be her husband? That story happened over a hundred years ago."

I was petrified. Was what Dan said true?

"How am I supposed to believe you're Franklin Brown?"

I continued, "Look at you. You're a twenty-nine-year-old male. You expect me to believe you're some geezer?"

"Oh this," he replied. "This is nothing. The idiot fell asleep on the job, and I just took over his body. It's a very simple process you see. Many losers get jobs at this cemetery, and amongst them are people that are lazy, or overworked and tired. They fall asleep and I possess their bodies."

He continued, "Obviously, I couldn't use my real name, so I used my middle name Daniel. I've spent numerous bodies in search of this here beauty."

Dan or "Franklin" put his arm around Samantha, who was frozen in fear. I felt bad for her. She wasn't able to escape that psychopath even after a hundred years.

"Well, it looks like she doesn't want to be with you," I said, regretting such a dumb decision. "You murdered her, why would she want to stay with you?"

"Shut up," Franklin said, his face red. "Mind your own business. That's the problem with this new generation. You all want to stick your faces in on family matters."

"It's not sticking our faces in other people's family matters. I'm roped in this too now. And I'm just as uncomfortable, as a matter of fact, not at the level she is with how you're acting."

Samantha looked up, she looked thankful a stranger would help her. I nodded at her before looking back to Franklin. His arm still locked around her waist. The situation was becoming more and more dangerous, for me and possibly more for her.

"I see what this is," Franklin understood. "You're after my wife. Is that it? Why you're so against her being with me. Making up lies, claiming she doesn't want me."

The situation escalated quickly, "What? No. What in the world would make you think I fell for a ghost?"

I continued, "She's dead, no reason for me to like her. I can tell that she is afraid of you. In your stories you acknowledged that you were abusive, and that you murdered her. On what planet would a woman who ran away come back?"

Through his enraged reaction Franklin's arm lowered from her waist. It gave her the chance she needed to leave. I glanced over at the moveable Samantha, who made it clear she would run for it. So, I decided to keep Franklin distracted as she made her escape.

"What about the priest? Whenever he comes, is that because you know you're not strong enough to go against him?"

"Ha," he laughed insanely. "You think he has a chance against me? I disappear because I don't want anything to do with that disgusting place."

"What happens to the men you possess after you leave their body? They can't just continue life as is. if you don't think that you're a cruel person, explain that."

"I'm not cruel," his reply was smug. "When I leave their bodies, I simply kill them. They don't know what hit them."

I looked to see if Samantha left, and it appeared so. Franklin noticed I was looking around for something, and realized Samantha was gone.

"Where is she," he was furious. "Where did she go!"

He grabbed my shoulders with immense force.

"I don't know," I spat out. "I was focused on arguing with you to notice her leave."

He let go of me and started looking around the headstone.

"Well you're going to help me find her. I spent too much time searching for her to let her go for some piece of shit."

"Okay," I responded.

It wouldn't have mattered anyways, I would have just left when we separated and found the priest. We searched until dawn, he was pissed.

"Where the hell could she have gone? She must be stuck in this cemetery."

Franklin kicked some rocks before parking himself on a gravestone.

"Look," I mumbled. "You wasted so much time on a dead girl, why don't you find someone better. Women today are greater than women from your time period."

"No," he said, sharply. "Women of this time period aren't even women. They're men. You can't even get a basic meal from them."

"But you believe Samantha was?"

"Yes, she was obedient. She knew her place."

"Well, it looks like she's gone. She might not be stuck here. And now that she knows you're here, she may never comeback. Why waste another century or two searching for her?"

He looked at me, as if something had gotten through.

"I know what we'll do," he stood up. "Instead of just me searching for her, you will too."

"What? Like hell I'll help a murderous lunatic find his wife who doesn't want to be found."

"Oh, you will," he confirmed. "This is your fault for sticking your nose in someone else's business. You'll stick your nose into finding her."

"How, unlike you, I'm alive."

"Not anymore," he said, before shoving something sharp into my chest.

Blood came out of my mouth, I looked down at the large stick shoved into my chest before I could come to the fact I was dying. I looked at Franklin once more before everything turned black.

I came to, as if nothing happened.

"I knew it would work," Franklin stated as he stepped away from me.

"You killed me?!" I shouted.

"Yep, and you're stuck to me forever," he said, a huge grin was plastered on his face. "Enjoy the life of the dead."

A couple of decades passed since then, and we still haven't found Samantha. I've tried many times to let the priest know, but it's hard to go into the church. So, when I'm not searching for her, I spend my time trying to scare unsuspecting workers from entering the cemetery. This story is just to warn you, not to work in a cemetery, or trust those who do.

CHAPTER FOURTEEN
A WALK BACK FROM THE OTHER SIDE

My life with Esmerelda was amazing. I couldn't have asked for more. But I just couldn't stop thinking I was forgetting something. For most of the time, Esmerelda begged me never to leave the house and I followed her command. What kind of husband would I be if I let her down?

But one day, everything changed. Esmerelda left the house at her usual time, and I was alone when I heard a child cry. It was rare to see children in this area, so it was definitely odd to see her standing there. Was she another Nymph or something else? I knew Esmerelda would be disappointed in me for doing this, but I couldn't leave the child by herself. I walked outside. The smell of the forest was nostalgic. I missed being in the fresh air.

"Are you okay?" I asked walking to her.

"I can't find my mommy," she wailed.

"It's okay. I'll take you to her. Okay?"

She nodded.

"Do you remember where she was? Do you know where your house is?"

"Yeah," she sniffed.

"Okay, let's go. I'm sure she's waiting there for you."

We walked for hours, deeper and deeper into the woods.

"How much farther?" I asked.

"Not much, we almost there."

I looked ahead to a faint light in the distance. It was a cottage.

"Is your mom there? I'll head back now."

"No," she shouted. "Please come with me."

"Are you still scared?"

She nodded and held my hand.

We walked to door and my head ached. I was being told something, I needed to go inside to know what. When we entered, my head pounded.

"Do you remember now?" the little girl asked.

"Remember what?" I moaned.

"Who you really are?"

The little girl transformed into a horrendous creature. I winced at its ugliness.

"What are you?" I asked.

"Do you really not remember me? I am Maurelle, a Sprite that came to warn you of your wife's trickery."

"My 'wife's trickery?'"

"Yes, you not remember where you're from. Who you used to be. But I came to help you."

"I know exactly where I came from. And who I am. I'm leaving."

"Wait," Maurelle said. "Please, have a bite. I am a lonely Sprite. I know no friends and today I just need someone to celebrate my birthday with. Please at least partake in some cake. This will be the first anyone has ever shared a cake with me."

Though she disrespected my wife, I couldn't leave her to be alone on her birthday. It was a lonely feeling.

"Just one slice," I said, as Maurelle handed over a piece.

I took a bite of the cake, and it was horrible. Maurelle could tell I didn't like it, it was obvious on my face.

"You don't like it?" she asked.

"It's just...very sweet," I lied. I continued to eat. It would be rude to spit it out.

Once I finished, I felt strange. I became dizzy, the room and Maurelle began to spin, and I fainted.

When I came to, Maurelle stood over me.

"Flunky?" I asked groggy.

"Flunky?"

"Nothing."

"You remember now?"

"Yeah, thanks. But neither of you are getting me." I kicked Maurelle out of the way.

She snarled, and I ran out the door. I wasn't heading back to Esmerelda either. I ran back to the field. The door was still there but covered in vines. I was heading home when Maurelle appeared from behind.

"You'll pay for that," she growled. Her form now a monster.

I was close to the door, not even 10ft away when Esmerelda appeared from behind it. As I got closer, tears were in her eyes.

"Are you really leaving me?" she asked.

"I need to go home. I already have a family."

"You can live a peaceful life here. Were you not annoyed with your wife?"

"I was but that doesn't mean I hate her."

I could hear Maurelle approaching faster.

"*Shit,*" I thought leaping for the doorknob.

When I touched the handle, a bright light shined and Esmerelda and Maurelle were gone. I looked around for them, but they were nowhere nearby, and I wasn't going to wait for them to show up again. I looked down, I was finally going home. I took my first step through the door, and everything went dark.

I opened my eyes to the cold snow. The blizzard had ended just as I opened my eyes. I was freezing, I could barely move. But I wanted to get as far away as I could from that place. I shivered as I got onto my knees, I was moving on sheer willpower alone. I made it to my feet and slowly walked in the other direction of where I faced.

I was finally heading back. Back to Jannette, back to Katie and Mark, back to reality. As I thought about them, it was just my luck a ranger was on patrol. I could barely speak, I tried so hard to get my voice. I mustered up all I could and shouted.

"Hey, over here," I hollered. I saw the brake lights and yelled louder. "Help! I'm over here!"

The ranger pulled around to me, "You Bill Dauber?"

"Yeah," I said.

"I been lookin' for you. Hop in," he said, unlocking the doors.

I crawled in back, and the moment the heat hit me, chills ran down my spine. I was so cold I forgot what warmth felt like. I took a deep breath and relaxed in the seat.

The drive was no longer than 5 minutes. I was closer to the cabin than I thought. When we arrived, Jannette jumped into my arms crying. She was apologizing profusely, and I just held her close.

I was seen by a doctor, who said I was lucky to be alive. I was diagnosed with severe frostbite. He insisted I went to the hospital, but I didn't want to be anywhere but there.

After everything died down, I apologized to Jannette for my behavior.

"I'm really sorry," I said, grabbing Jannette's hand. "I was a complete asshole for what I did. If there's any way you could forgive me...."

Jannette placed her hand on my cheek, "Shh, I'm not mad. I'm glad you're alive. It was my fault too. I shouldn't have provoked you and broken your laptop."

"It's alright," I smiled. "I must be very delirious. You probably wouldn't believe what happened to me."

"What?" she asked.

"When I was out there, there was this door and I walked inside. It was an actual forest. And there was this Sprite and Nymph who fought over me. One wanted to eat me, the other was in love with me," I sighed. "It was a complete mess. Heh, you probably think I'm crazy."

I looked over at Jannette who sat with her hand covering her mouth, "What were their names?"

"U-Um, Esmerelda and Maurelle."

Realization hit Jannette's face, and she said, "I am soo so so so sorry. Esmerelda is my aunt and Maurelle is her friend. I told them what happened between us when you left, and I guess they decided to take things into their own hand. No wonder you were able to survive."

"So, you're telling me, I went through a lot of stress because of your aunt," I slid deeper into the bed.

"I'm sorry."

"It's fine, you know you don't look much like your aunt. So, you're a Nymph?"

"Sort of, I'm half human. My father was a Nymph, my mother human. You aren't surprised?"

"After what Esmerelda did, nothing surprises me anymore."

I kissed Jannette and closed my eyes, "Your aunt isn't allowed at family gatherings for a long time."

Author's Note

I hope you liked A Walk on the Other Side. I would say 3 or 4 of the stories were written in a creative writing class in high school and college. I really enjoyed them and the stories from high school were the, I guess you would say "kick starter" for this book. The first story was the Creature, it was written for a Halloween story my junior year of high school. It was supposed to be just for fun, but I received a lot of praise for it and kept the file. The next was The Ornament, it was the second assignment. It was around Christmas when it was assigned so I made it about Christmas. Again, I receive 100% and a lot of praise and decided to keep it. After that I began to read more of Stephen King and other authors which made me want to write more.

Watching television shows like Twilight Zone, Goosebumps and the Haunting Hour by R.L Stine gave me the motivation and set the mood to write eerie stories as well as listening to Lucas King's compositions (a youtuber from the UK. *VERY* amazing pianist/composer, whose works made it easier to write).

I was hoping with these stories it would give the reader different kinds of emotions. For example, Dr. Vogel and Johann's stories were meant to make you sad, and maybe different interpretations on humans and life. It was certainly something I wasn't used to. I wanted to give them a happy ending. The Cursed Boy was the first story I wrote with a happy ending. It was definitely weird. Lol.

For Insanity I was trying for a little scary and some sympathy for the boy (that alone should be enough, I didn't even give him a name lol. Feel free to give him one if you want.)

And for Ghost, I was hoping for a reaction towards "What the hell did I just read?" Haha.

How did you interpret the stories? What do you think the meaning behind each story was? If you thought it had one that is.

A friend of mine had a completely different understanding for Insanity than I intended.

Thank you for your support reading this!

A.J.